RIDING *the* FLUME

Also by Patricia Curtis Pfitsch

Keeper of the Light

The Deeper Song

PATRICIA CURTIS PFITSCH

RIDING
the FLUME

Aladdin Paperbacks
New York   London   Toronto   Sydney

First Aladdin Paperbacks edition April 2004
Copyright © 2002 by Patricia Curtis Pfitsch

ALADDIN PAPERBACKS
An imprint of Simon & Schuster
Children's Publishing Division
1230 Avenue of the Americas
New York, NY 10020

Also available in a Simon & Schuster Books for Young Readers
hardcover edition
Designed by Interrobang Design Studio
The text of this book was set in Galliard.

Printed in the United States of America
2 4 6 8 10 9 7 5 3 1

The Library of Congress has cataloged the hardcover edition as
follows:
Pfitsch, Patricia Curtis
Riding the flume / by Particia Curtis Pfitsch.
p. cm.
Summary: In 1894, fifteen-year-old Francie
determines to fight the lumbermen and protect
the largest sequoia tree ever seen which had been given
to her sister just before her death six years earlier.
ISBN 0-689-83823-9 (hc.)
[1. Giant sequoia—Fiction. 2. Logging—Fiction. 3. Conservation
of natural resources—Fiction. 4. Frontier and pioneer life-
California—Fiction. 5. Depressions—1893—Fiction. 6. Sequoia
National Park (Calif.)—Fiction] I. Title.
PZ7.P4485585 Ri 2002
[Fic]—dc21 2001042948
ISBN 0-689-86692-5 (Aladdin pbk.)

To Jack, who sees Truth in contradictions

· Acknowledgments ·

Writing may be a solitary occupation, but each book depends not only on the author's imagination, but also on the help and goodwill of other people. I want to thank my agent, George Nicholson, and my editor, David Gale, both for their confidence in me and for their sound writing advice.

Thanks to the members of my critique group for their unfailing support and their extreme patience in reading these chapters in their roughest form. And last, but certainly not least, thanks to my family. You are the foundation upon which I'm able to build my dreams, and the most important part of everything I do.

Readers always ask me whether the places and people in my novels are real. In the case of *Riding the Flume,* the setting bears a conscious and yet not-exact resemblance to the area west of Kings Canyon and Sequoia National Parks

in California. Connorsville and St. Joseph are made-up
towns, and Connor's Basin is also an imaginary place.
However, one of the longest lumber flumes ever built had
its beginning point in Millwood, California, a town that
no longer exists but that used to lie northwest of what is
now Kings Canyon National Park. This flume carried lumber out of the mountains down to Sanger, a small town
east of Fresno, California. It was fifty-four miles long,
twenty miles longer than the lumber flume I've created for
Riding the Flume, but not as dangerous to ride. As for the
people, no character in this book bears any intentional
resemblance to any real person, living or dead.

· Prologue ·

All week the Sierra Lumber Company's best axmen had swung their double-bitted axes, chopping little by little into the spongy red bark and then the bright, fragrant heartwood of the ancient sequoia tree. It had seemed impossible, like two ants taking tiny bites out of a tall man's ankle. How could something so small as a man with an ax conquer something so huge as a giant sequoia? But it had been done before. The sound of the chopping was sharp and steady in the clear mountain air.

As soon as the axmen had made a huge seven-foot-high notch in the trunk, the sawyers had gone to work on the other side of the tree. They'd already welded two crosscut saws together to make one long saw about twenty-five feet long. Two men each took one end of the saw. Its sharp teeth looked like a monstrous giant's grin.

From where the sawyers stood they couldn't even see

the notch, a dark and weeping wound on the other side of the tree. Back and forth they drew the saw, and it slowly slid into the bark. The sawyers made it seem easy, but it was clear from the sweat running down their faces that it was much harder than it looked. Deeper and deeper the saw sank into the tree until it had almost reached the notch. And then the sawyers stopped.

The felling of the first sequoia in Connor's Basin was going to be an event for the whole town to celebrate. Thomas Connor would see to that. The top of his carriage was visible over the crowd as he led the townspeople to the grove—they came in buggies, in wagons, and on foot. Nobody wanted to miss it.

A small platform had been hastily built not far from the dying giant. Thomas Connor gestured, and his driver pulled the carriage up beside the platform. Connor stepped from the carriage, straightened the coat of his neat black suit, and then turned to help his wife and his daughter, seating them on the chairs waiting for them on the platform. Mrs. Connor's face was hidden by the dark veil of her wide-brimmed hat. Her fancy dress, with its full skirts and puffed sleeves, would have been out of place here in the woods on a regular day, but today was as special as the Fourth of July.

Thomas Connor raised his arms over his head, and the noisy chatter of the crowd died away. The woods were empty for once of the pounding of axes, the crash of trees falling, the screeching of the logs as they were dragged along in the wooden chutes to the mill, and the shouts and curses of the lumbermen. It was so silent the people could actually hear the birds calling and twittering in the branches of the trees hundreds of feet overhead.

"We are gathered here today to celebrate the beginning of the Sierra Lumber Company's most daring venture." Connor's loud voice was a bit muffled among the great trees, as if their fibrous bark was absorbing the sound. "I am here to put the rumors to rest. Far from being on the edge of bankruptcy as some have claimed, we are now stronger than ever." He gestured around him. "Here you see the latest in technology, engineering, and the genius of mankind. Yes, bringing all this together in one place has been expensive. And I am proud of all the loyal lumbermen who were willing, even eager, to give up their weekly paychecks to make this possible."

Some of the loggers nodded, their faces glowing. But others frowned. Sometimes when the paychecks were withheld, there were near riots in the lumber camp. But not many quit; with the depression on, jobs were few and far between.

"Eager, my foot," grumbled old Ben. He took his unlit cigar from his mouth and spit onto the ground. He'd been one of the finest axmen of his time, everyone said, but now his fingers were so knotted with rheumatism he could barely hold an ax. This year he'd been hired on as foreman of the crew; his hands didn't work anymore, but there was nothing wrong with his voice.

"Now all our efforts have come to fruition." Connor raised his voice a notch over the grumbles. "Each tree in this grove will yield as much as six hundred thousand board feet of lumber—enough to build forty complete houses." He turned, surveyed the grove, and looked again at his audience. "All the houses in the great state of California could come from this very grove. Citizens of Connorsville, your future looks bright. And to prove it to you, I'm going to raise every salary fifteen cents a day, starting today!"

Cheers and whistles erupted from the crowd, and some of the men threw their caps in the air. Fifteen cents!

"Huh!" Old Ben grumbled again. "Easy enough to owe a dollar and fifteen cents a day as to owe a dollar," he growled.

"Now, if you people will be so good as to stand back," Connor was saying, "we'll bring this old giant down and start earning our fifteen-cent raise." He offered his hand first to his wife and then to his daughter, helping them into the waiting carriage. He stepped in and the carriage moved away, followed by the townspeople—a human river flowing down the hill and up to a rise about two hundred feet away.

Throughout the week, as the giant saw had been moving closer and closer to the notch, other men had been hammering huge steel wedges into the slice made by the blade. This kept the enormous weight of the tree from trapping the saw forever in the middle of the giant trunk. Now, at Connor's signal, more wedges were hammered into the ever-widening crack, forcing the tree to lean in the proper direction. The minutes crawled by and the ringing of ax on steel continued, filling the air with the tuneless pounding. Then, majestically, the ancient tree began to topple. At first it seemed as if a slight breeze was ruffling the leaves, which were almost out of sight at the top of the tree. The trunk began to sway and creak, and then to lean, slowly at first and then faster and faster. Popping and cracking louder than gunshots, the enormous trunk hurtled toward the earth. It hit the forest floor with the force of an explosion, as if they'd blasted half the mountainside away with a ton of gunpowder. The woods were suddenly engulfed in a thick brown cloud, and then dust and debris began to shower down like rain.

On the rise where the crowd had gathered to watch the show, men began cheering and whistling. But as the dust slowly cleared, the cheers died and silence settled on the forest. The bulk of the tree could be seen stretched out on the ground. The giant trunk, once as wide as many of the houses in Connorsville were tall, had shattered into thousands of useless pieces.

Deep within the stump, a shudder was vibrating the wood, as if in reaction to sudden emptiness after centuries of carrying the weight of the giant tree. "It's shaking," someone cried out. "The stump is shaking."

"Clear these people away!" Connor's voice was urgent and angry, and the lumbermen began directing the towns-people back to Connorsville. So began the logging of Connor's Basin.

· Chapter One ·

Francie Cavanaugh lay flat on her stomach on the top of the old sequoia stump. A slight breeze billowed her skirt out around her legs and the toes of her old high-buttoned shoes pointed straight into the wood. She kept her finger firmly pressed against the 2,500th ring while she lay her head down, resting her neck. She could feel the heat of the rough sun-warmed wood against her cheek and smell the tangy-sweet scent of resin. "Twenty-five hundred years," she whispered. And she wasn't to the center yet—there were probably at least five hundred rings left to count.

That meant the tree had been growing for three thousand years when Connor and his men had cut it down six years ago. She sat up, but kept her finger on the tree ring. "What was happening three thousand years ago?" she asked a robin who had come to perch on the upright pole of the ladder leaning against the giant stump. He seemed totally unafraid of her. He cocked his head and examined her with one bright black eye as if to say, "Well, out with it!"

She answered slowly, thinking it out as if she were in school. "This is the year of our Lord 1894. It was almost two thousand years ago that Jesus was born." She sucked in her breath. The tree had been over a thousand years old at the time of Christ! Maybe it had sprouted around the time Moses was leading the Hebrews through the wilderness. It was almost too much to imagine. With her free hand she stroked the wood gently as if the stump could feel her touch. But she knew it couldn't feel her. She closed her eyes. It was dead now. Like Carrie. She shook that thought away before the lump could form in her throat and leaned down to resume counting.

"Francie!" It was her mother's voice. She was coming up the path. Francie looked around, realizing too late that the sun was close to setting. She'd lost track of the time again! She grabbed the sharp stone near her hand and scratched two lines across the 2,500th ring to mark her place. Then she stood and looked down, past the swelling buttresses around the bottom of the stump, to the ground. The loggers had started their cut about twenty feet up where the trunk was thinner, so she was way too high up to jump. She sighed and swung herself onto the ladder.

She had to place her feet carefully to avoid the broken rungs as she climbed down. "No wonder the loggers left it here when they moved," she grumbled, hoping her mother wouldn't notice how rickety it was.

Even if a rung looked solid, she tested it before she stepped on it. She took another step, and just as she'd decided it was safe to put her whole weight on the rung, it snapped with a loud cracking sound. The ladder started to teeter, but Francie's fingers found a hole in the bark of the old stump. She gripped hard at the hole and kept the ladder upright.

Blessing the animal who'd made the hole, Francie shifted her weight until the ladder leaned solidly against the stump once again. "Maybe it was an owl," she said, slowly uncurling her fingers, ready to grab again if the ladder moved.

The ladder held firm, but as Francie let go of the edge of the hole she felt something brush her fingertips. She fought the urge to jerk her hand away. Maybe it was a baby bird, she thought. A baby owl. Slowly she took a step up so she could get a glimpse into the hole.

Sunlight shone obligingly into the blackness, but what Francie saw was not an animal but a small cloth bag.

Francie could hear her mother's voice getting louder. In a moment she would reach the clearing. Quickly Francie drew the bag out of the hole. It was made of oiled cloth to make it waterproof and was so light, Francie thought there couldn't be anything inside. She wiggled her fingers into the opening and pulled it wide.

There was something inside after all, a folded piece of paper. She hooked her arm around the ladder, took the paper out of the bag, and unfolded it.

> **Meet me at Turkey Fork**
> **half past four on Sunday.**
> **Don't tell anyone—the only safety is in secrecy.**

The handwriting was almost illegible. Francie's heart gave an unexpected lurch that made her momentarily dizzy. She didn't understand the meaning of the words, but she knew very well who had written the message. The barely readable handwriting had to be her sister Carrie's.

"Francie!" Her mother stood with her hands on her hips and looked up at her daughter. "How many times . . ." she began.

Francie shifted so her body was covering the hole and shoved the bag and message back inside. She could only hope that her mother hadn't seen it. She took a deep breath, willing her heart to slow down, trying to look like nothing had happened. She glanced down at the top of her mother's head. Her shining hair gleamed in the last rays of the evening sun, and it was all still pinned neatly in place. Her mother had walked all the way from town, and Francie knew she'd been working all day in the hotel, but her dark brown skirt and white shirtwaist looked as fresh as if she'd just dressed. "I know," Francie said. "You don't have to tell me."

"I think I do," her mother answered, steadying the ladder as Francie made her way down. "You must not be listening. I've told you over and over that I don't want you to come here, but here you are."

Francie hopped from the lowest rung, climbing over the bulging roots of the ancient stump. She grabbed the ladder and lowered it to the ground, grateful that her mother's eyes seemed to be fixed on her and not the broken rungs of the ladder. "The loggers are working miles away from here, Mama," she said. She searched her mother's face for signs of anger but found only a kind of patient sadness that made Francie's heart twist painfully. She wanted somehow to assure her mother there wasn't any danger, but she knew it was hopeless. Her mother would always think the woods were dangerous.

Francie placed her hand on the side of the huge tree stump. "Mr. Court asked me to count the rings of this old stump last month when he was staying at the hotel. He wanted to know how old it was when they cut it down. I've got to twenty-five hundred, and I'm not done yet." She carefully kept her eyes away from the hole. She wanted to examine the message in private, without her mother looking over her shoulder.

"Mercy!" Her mother took a closer look at the tree stump. "Twenty-five hundred years old?"

"More than that," Francie said. "Maybe three thousand or even older."

Her mother shook her head and clicked her tongue against her teeth. "It's a shame," she said almost under her breath. "Even if Thomas Connor's money is practically keeping the hotel in business, it's still a shame."

The two of them turned away from the stump and headed down the path toward town. "Your father will be back from St. Joseph tonight, and I don't want anything to upset him," her mother said, giving Francie a pointed look.

In other words, thought Francie, her mother didn't want her father to know she had gone to the basin again. Both her parents thought it was too close to the logging operation, too dangerous, even though the loggers had moved way over to the east end of the basin two years ago.

She probably shouldn't mention Mr. Court, the newspaperman, either, and the promise she'd made to him. Mr. Court had spent most of his week in the mountains tramping around in the woods and observing the logging operation. "I'm going to run a series of articles on the Sierra Lumber Company," he told Francie when she'd summoned the courage to ask him about it one evening. He was a quiet man with a shy smile, but his eyes looked like they could see right inside you. Francie thought she would not want to make him angry.

When Mr. Court had arrived, everyone expected he would write about the great work of the lumber company, supplying wood for homes across the nation. Father wasn't so welcoming when he found out Mr. Court was against the logging, though he could hardly ask him to leave the hotel. But Father certainly wouldn't be happy to learn that Mr. Court had enlisted Francie's aid in learning more about the sequoias.

Francie watched her mother pick her way carefully along the path and wondered what she really thought about the logging. Father was in favor of it, of course. And she knew from her father's grumbling that there were more and more people like Mr. Court who were against it. Her mother would never contradict her father, Francie knew that. But in her own heart, did her mother think it was wrong to cut the big trees?

Francie stopped on the rise and looked back into the basin. Here and there a sequoia had been left standing. They even looked ancient, she thought. Their tops were rounded, worn down by the centuries. Their branches were twisted like old Ben's arthritic fingers, but they seemed calm and majestic as if they'd seen too much of life to be surprised at anything. And these were the smaller trees and the ones that grew on the hillside in such a way that the loggers already knew they could never be felled without shattering. The broken trunks of the really big trees littered the field before her—these were the ones that shattered when they fell or when the loggers tried to blast them into pieces small enough to transport to the mill. Sequoia stumps filled the area like the enormous footprints of some monster hopping willy-nilly through the mountains. From here they didn't look that big, she thought, but she knew better. There was a stump up north that had been used as a dance floor—it was said that thirty couples were able to dance on it at one time. And these stumps were bigger than that one. She squinted her eyes almost shut, trying to remember what it had been like before the Sierra Lumber Company had moved in.

She must have followed Carrie here, trailing behind her as she'd wandered among the trees. She didn't remember seeing her sister put messages in that hole, but it would have been like Carrie to do it. She had followed her sister everywhere in those days, keeping up as best she could, watching Carrie ride the wildest horse, hike the hardest trail, climb the highest tree. Carrie had known the names of all the plants that grew in the mountains and all the animals who lived there. Carrie had made it to the summit of any mountain she decided to climb. "You can see to the end of the world," she'd tell Francie when she returned. She'd laugh when Francie would fall off her pony or stumble over her own baby feet on a level path. "You'd better stay away from the top of the mountain," she'd tease. "You're sure to fall off."

Francie shook the memories away. "But I'm still here," she whispered. She turned and followed her mother back to town.

• • •

It was just plain bad luck that brought James Cavanaugh along the road from St. Joseph at the very time that Francie and her mother were hurrying back from Connor's Basin. They heard the quick trot of horses' hooves behind them and stepped off the rutted dirt road to let the rider pass. But instead he pulled up beside them.

"What are you doing out here?" Francie's father asked. "Who's watching the hotel desk?" His mare, always a little skittish, sidestepped at the noise and the irritated jerks he gave to the reins. He looked down at his wife. "She's been at the basin again, hasn't she, Mary?"

"Herbert can manage very well." Francie's mother answered his first questions but ignored his last. "After all, that's why we hired a desk clerk, isn't it?" She looked down and brushed off her skirt with restless fingers. "We've only been gone for a few minutes."

Francie's father gave a short, mirthless laugh. "You may have been gone only a few moments, but I'll wager Frances has been away most of the afternoon." He looked at her. "Is that right, daughter?"

Francie sighed. "I was counting the rings of that old stump—you know, the first one they cut in the grove." She raised her chin. "Mr. Court asked me to find out how old the tree was. I've counted 2,500 rings so far, and I'm not done yet." She saw a flicker of interest cross her father's face, but it died instantly.

"Yes, well, we did know those trees were old—that's

why they're so big." He gave her a hard look. "But you know very well I don't want you wandering alone in these mountains." He touched his heels to the mare's sides and moved his hand up on her neck. "We'll talk about this at supper," he said over his shoulder as the mare trotted on toward Connorsville.

Francie and her mother exchanged a look. "I'm sorry, Mama," Francie whispered. "I really wasn't doing anything dangerous."

Her mother sighed. "I know," she said. "But he worries so much about you."

Francie shrugged. That wasn't quite the way she'd describe it, but it would help nothing to get into that argument now. Francie followed her mother to town and thought instead about how soon she could get back to take a better look at that message.

· Chapter Two ·

Even before she stepped into the kitchen, Francie could smell the stew her mother had left simmering on the stove. The rich odor of beef and potatoes made her mouth water.

"Please set the table," Francie's mother said, tying her apron on over her skirt.

"Yes, ma'am," Francie answered. She went to the cupboard and brought plates and silver to the table, but after one look at her father's grim face as he sat waiting for the meal, her eagerness for supper faded. She laid the places in silence and was careful not to meet her father's eyes.

Francie helped her mother carry the steaming dishes into the dining room, and at her mother's signal, took her chair. She watched as her mother ladled potatoes, carrots, and chunks of tender beef onto her plate, but worry sat like a stone in her stomach, and she knew she would not be able to eat.

"For what we are about to receive," her father prayed, bowing his head and folding his hands, "may the Lord make us truly grateful."

"Amen," murmured Francie and her mother. Francie kept her head bowed and watched out of the corner of her eye. After her mother took the first bite, Francie and her father could begin to eat. For too many long minutes, the only sound at the table was the gentle clink as silver touched china. Francie picked up a roll, broke it into pieces, and began nibbling on one corner.

She jumped as her father put down his fork and cleared his throat. "Frances," he began, "please explain to me why it was so important for you to visit the basin today against our wishes."

Francie put the roll down on her plate. "I'd promised Mr. Court, Father. He's writing an article on the sequoias for his paper." She met her father's eyes. "I couldn't break my promise."

Francie's father frowned. "So instead you broke our rules."

"But, Father," Francie said, "this is important."

Her father's frown grew darker. "And our rules are not?"

Francie bit her lip. "That's not what I meant," she said. She took a breath. "What I meant is that Mr. Court is going to write an article for his newspaper. He wants to stop the logging of the sequoias. He thinks it's a waste."

She leaned forward, her eyes on his face. "It is a waste, Father. You know it is."

Her father picked up his napkin and placed it beside his plate. "What I know is that the logging has kept us in business," her father said, his voice turning hard.

Francie saw her mother's warning look, but she couldn't stop. "Mr. Court says they could log the other trees that don't take so long to grow and leave the sequoias," she persisted.

"Each one of those big trees can supply enough wood to build forty, five-room houses, Frances! They're our economic future!" He shook his head. "I will hear no more talk about it. And you may not go to Connor's Basin anymore," he added. "It's entirely too dangerous for a young girl."

"You let Carrie go anywhere she wanted to," Francie burst out before she could stop herself. Even hearing that name caused her parents such pain that her sister was rarely mentioned in the household.

Her father's face turned pale. *I've gone too far this time*, Francie thought. But she couldn't go back now.

"That was entirely different," her father said. His voice had sunk almost to a whisper. "Carrie was capable . . ."

Francie dug her fingernails into her palms under the table, and the prick of pain reminded her to hold her tongue. She took a deep breath. "Father, I'm careful," she said, trying to keep her voice low. "That's what I've learned since the landslide. I don't take risks."

She looked up at his blank face—his eyes were dull and without emotion. She knew it wasn't any use. She pushed back her chair and stood up, the anger boiling up inside her like a volcano. "I'll never be as perfect as your wonderful Carrie, will I, Father?" Hot tears sprang to her eyes, but she ignored them and kept staring at his flat, expressionless face. She wondered suddenly what it would take to bring some feeling back to him. How far would she have to go?

When she heard her mother's soft whimper, remorse washed over her. How could she be so cruel? She hung her head, but the words of apology didn't come.

There was a long silence. Then finally her father spoke. Even his voice sounded flat. "I don't think we need to continue this conversation any longer," he said. Carefully he folded his napkin and stood up. "My rule still stands. You may not go to Connor's Basin. Do you understand?" He glanced once at Francie's mother, as if making sure she, too, understood the rule. Then he straightened his waistcoat and left the room.

Francie stood with her head bowed, listening to her father's footsteps, hoping he'd come back. She heard the creak of the kitchen door as he opened it. There was a pause, as if he were standing in the doorway waiting, and her heart seemed to jump into her throat. But then the door slammed. She heard him go down the porch steps. He must be going back to his work at the hotel, she thought. He wasn't going to change his mind.

Her mother was leaning her head into her hands, and her shoulders were shaking. "Mama?" Francie knelt beside her mother's chair and put her hand on her arm. "Mama, I'm so sorry. I didn't mean to cause you pain." She sighed. "It's just . . ."

Her mother raised her head and wiped away her tears with her fingers. "Why do you anger him so?" she asked, touching her daughter's cheek. "If you just wouldn't provoke him, he wouldn't feel like he had to punish you."

Francie pulled her own chair next to her mother's and sat down. She clasped her hands in her lap. "He's angry that I'm helping Mr. Court," she whispered.

"He's worried about you," her mother said. "Can't you see that?"

"He's punishing me for Carrie's mistake," Francie retorted. "He can't hear a word said against her."

Her mother looked at Francie. "If you only knew how much you're growing to look like Carrie," she said, and her voice was soft. "How much you sound like her. Even when you argue with your father, you sound like her." Her mother looked away and a small smile came to her lips. She looked back at Francie. "Especially when you argue with your father," she added. "Don't you remember?"

Francie swallowed. "I remember," she whispered. She closed her eyes. Every time she looked in the mirror she remembered. It was why she'd cut her front hair in bangs and wore her back hair loose. It would have been so much more convenient to put it up in a bun like Carrie had worn her hair. But she couldn't stand the startled glances of her neighbors or the pain that crossed her father's face when he looked at her. She wiped away her tears with a corner of her napkin. Would she be forever in Carrie's shadow? In death as well as in life?

Her mother touched her cheek. "You would have been quite a pair, you know," she said. The words hung in the air for a long moment. Then Francie's mother pushed back her chair and stood up. "Josie?" she called to the young woman they'd hired to help around the house and the hotel. "Is the water hot?" She began collecting plates and cups and stacking them on the tray.

"Yes, ma'am," said Josie, appearing in the kitchen doorway with a towel in her hand. Francie's mother handed her the tray, and the two of them went into the kitchen.

It was Francie's job to put the rest of the tableware back on the sideboard and fold the napkins into their rings for the next meal. She did it absently, thinking about her mother's words. "Quite a pair," she'd said. Somehow Francie had never imagined herself and her sister as a "pair." How could they have ever been a pair, she thought. Carrie had been so much older—fifteen when she died, and Francie only nine. If Carrie had lived she'd be . . . Francie figured it out. Carrie would have been twenty-one. A woman grown. And Francie herself was only just fifteen now. How could she ever have caught up?

She threw the napkins into the basket with the others on the sideboard. She arranged the everyday salt and pepper shakers on the shelf with the ones for formal occasions and banged the cupboard door shut with more force than was necessary. "No," she said aloud. "I'll always be running behind her. Even now when she's dead."

She stomped up the stairs and plopped down in the chair by her vanity, carefully avoiding the oval mirror on the wall beside her. Her eyes fell instead on the framed photograph of the family, taken perhaps a year before the landslide. Father, sitting in the leather armchair in the parlor with the women gathered around him. Mother, in a dark dress with white buttons down the front and with an unfamiliar formal look on her face, her hand on her husband's shoulder. Francie, leaning against her father's knee. And Carrie, her long chestnut hair wound about her head in a complicated twist, was standing on Father's other side looking as if she wanted to laugh out loud.

Francie stared at the photograph, realizing again that anyone who didn't know the family might have taken Carrie for Francie. There was her sister, caught forever inside the little frame. And quietly, without thinking about it, the scrawny eight-year-old who had been leaning against her father's leg was, indeed, catching up. "In fact," she said aloud, finally looking at herself in the mirror, "I have caught up. I'm fifteen now, older than Carrie was then. She gathered her hair, twisted it, and wound it around her head, but immediately let it go. It was uncanny how much she looked like her sister.

"I wonder what it would have been like," she asked aloud, "if we'd been the same age." She picked up the deep blue cologne bottle on her vanity that used to be Carrie's and ran her fingers over the bumpy surface. She pulled the glass stopper out of the top and sniffed—the bottle had been empty for years. Carrie had given it to her long before the landslide. But the spicy smell of the cologne still lingered. "Would you have been my friend, Carrie?" she asked the picture. Carrie seemed to be looking out of the frame right into Francie's eyes. Her mouth held its almost smile. But the only answer was silence.

· Chapter Three ·

The only safety is in secrecy. The words hung in the air and Francie sat straight up in bed. She'd been dreaming. In the dream Francie had been standing at the bottom of the tallest part of the lumber flume, watching her sister climb up to the top. The night breeze fluttered Carrie's white nightgown and made Francie shiver. "Don't do it!" Francie called. She could feel her heart beating furiously in her chest. Something terrible was going to happen. "Please," Francie cried. "Please stop!"

Carrie looked down, hanging onto the wooden crosspiece with one hand. Her laugh was the same rippling musical sound that Francie had always loved. "I'm going to ride the flume," she called back, and kept climbing, step by step, to the top. Her arms and legs moved together in the easy, fluid movements that characterized everything Carrie did.

Now she had reached the top of the flume, so far away that she looked like a tiny white bird standing on the edge of the wooden track. She stretched her arms out wide, as if to embrace the star-studded sky. Her long hair streamed out behind her. Francie saw her climb into the flume boat and crouch down, gripping the sides with white fingers. Then the little wooden raft started to move, slowly at first. Francie sucked in her breath as it picked up speed, racing faster and faster down the track. Water splashed out on either side, cascading down the structure like a waterfall of sparkling diamonds.

"No!" Francie shouted. She tried to follow it, running below the little flume boat as it sped down the track. It was coming to the first sharp curve. If she could only get ahead, climb up, stop it somehow. . . .

She looked up as the boat hit the turn, bounced off the track, and went flying into the air. The scream stuck in her throat as she saw Carrie hold out her hands. "Remember," Carrie cried, "the only safety is in secrecy!"

Now, with the darkness engulfing her and her heart pounding, Francie wasn't sure if the words were in her dream or if she'd actually heard them spoken aloud. She fumbled with the matches and finally lit the candle she kept on her nightstand. She watched as the flickering light slowly brought the furniture into focus—the spindles flanking the foot of her bed, the wardrobe in the corner, the washstand and the white pitcher. Comforted by the light, she leaned back against her pillows. It was a stupid dream. Not even Carrie would have tried to ride the lumber flume—the thirty-mile track that floated the lumber out of the woods and down into the town of St. Joseph. It was too dangerous. She shook her head. A year ago Sean O'Brien and Buck Murphy, two of the biggest daredevils in the logging camp, had ridden it into St. Joseph—people had talked about it for months afterward. But Carrie would never have tried it.

But while the substance of the dream quickly faded, the feeling of guilt, of something she needed most urgently to do, lingered on. She couldn't remember the exact words of the message she'd found in the tree, except that part about the only safety being secrecy, but she thought it had communicated the same urgency. Something terrible about to happen, something someone had to stop.

But that had been six years ago. Who had the message been for? Who would have been meeting Carrie at Turkey Fork? Francie snuggled down under the covers. The answer to that, at least, was easy. If the note had not been meant for her cousin, Charlie, he would probably know who it *was* meant for. Carrie and Charlie had been best friends, even though Carrie had been two years older. If Charlie didn't know what Carrie had been talking about, then nobody would.

The raucous chorus of birds calling woke Francie just as the sky was beginning to turn pink. Summer was short in the high Sierras, and the birds didn't waste a moment of daylight. Francie's eyes still burned, and she was already tired, but she made herself get up. She didn't intend to waste any of the day, either. Her mother needed her in the hotel kitchen, but first she would talk to Charlie.

She pulled on an old dress, tied her apron over it, and tiptoed down the stairs. The house was silent—Mama and Father must still be in bed, she thought. Slowly she lifted the latch and opened the heavy front door—it moved smoothly on its hinges without even one squeak—and then she was out in the chilly dawn.

Across the narrow side street, her father's hotel loomed up twice as tall as any building around it. When they'd first moved to Connorsville, when Carrie was a baby, the family had actually lived in the hotel along with the guests, but when Francie was born, Mama had put her foot down and insisted they move to a real house.

Francie's old shoes made no sound in the dirt as she ran along the street. She turned the corner onto Main and glanced up, wishing as she often did that she could have a room on the top floor of the hotel. She would have a bird's-eye view of the whole town and the woods beyond; it would be almost like a tree house. But she knew better than to suggest it—she had heard her mother say often enough that owning a hotel was one thing; living in it was quite another.

She hurried down Main Street past the general store,

the post office, and the hospital and doctor's office. Lamps were being lit in the buildings now, and she could hear the rumble of voices and the clatter of pots and pans in the dining hall where the loggers were eating breakfast. They were at work by six o'clock, so they were up even earlier than the birds.

"Hey, Francie!"

She looked up to see Charlie take off his hat and wave from the dining hall porch. He crossed the street in three big strides and stopped in front of her, blocking her path. "Where are you headed so early, pretty lady? Looking for me, I hope?" He flashed her his famous winning smile, but he put his hands on her shoulders as if she were his little sister.

Francie blushed anyway. Her cousin, Charlie Spencer, was nineteen and so handsome he could have his pick of any girl in town. He was dressed for work—Francie recognized his red plaid flannel shirt and saw that it still had a hole in the elbow. "Hi, Charlie," she said. She knew he was being nice to her only because of Carrie, but she really was glad to see him. "I'd heard you made it back for another season after all. We thought you'd given up logging altogether when you didn't show up last week."

"No chance of that," he said. "This is the year I'm going to ride the flume!"

Francie laughed. "You say that every year."

Charlie winked at her and ran his fingers through his curly hair, making it stick up even more than usual.

"Actually, I'm headed out to Camp Four this morning— that's where we're working now. I'm just glad they were willing to hire me back on."

Francie chuckled. "Who else would they get to be chute rider?" She shook her head. "You probably could ride the flume. You're the only one who actually enjoys risking your life like that."

"Not the only one," Charlie said, grinning. He clapped his hat back on his head. "Where are you headed so early in the morning?" he asked again. "May I walk with you?" He offered her his arm.

She took a breath. "Actually, I was looking for you."

"I knew it!" Charlie crowed, and the two loggers who had followed him out of the dining hall grinned and poked each other.

Again, he proffered his crooked elbow and Francie rested her hand lightly on his arm. "It's not what you think," she said. "It's about Carrie."

Charlie's face turned sober. "Carrie?" He gave her an uneasy glance. "She's haunting me." Francie didn't know she'd said it out loud until she saw Charlie's startled face.

"What?" She saw his Adam's apple go up and down as he swallowed.

"Never mind. I'm just being silly." She took Charlie's arm again and they began to walk back in the direction of the hotel. "I have to ask you a question. But you have to promise not to tell anyone."

"Fire away," Charlie said, his eyes sparkling again. "I won't tell." He pushed on his hat brim so his hat perched on the back of his head.

Quickly she told him about the message in the old sequoia stump. "Was it for you? Did you and Carrie leave messages in that old tree hole?"

Charlie's eyes had a faraway look. "I'd forgotten about that," he said. "Carrie called it the post office. She liked it that we could say we were going to the post office and nobody would know what we meant. We were each supposed to check there every day, just the way people check their post office boxes." He looked down at Francie, and a slow smile touched his lips. "I used to get mad at her because she'd write messages about things she could just as well have told me in person. But that was your sister all over. Anything to make life more mysterious. What did it say again?"

Francie shook her head. "I only got a quick look before Mama came. Something about meeting at Turkey Fork. And then it said, 'The only safety is in secrecy.' That part I do remember. You mean you never got it?"

Charlie shook his head. "After the landslide . . ." He looked almost angry. "Well, what would have been the point? It busted me up enough as it was."

Francie nodded. "That means I was the first one to see it." They were almost to the hotel. She could see lights in the lobby, and Mama moving about in the kitchen across the street. She tugged on Charlie's arm until he stopped walking. "What do you think it means?"

"The message?" Charlie shrugged. "Let me have a look at it."

Francie drew a line in the dust with the toe of her shoe. "It's still in the tree, and I'm not allowed to go into the basin."

"You're not allowed?" Charlie shoved his hands into his pockets. "Why not?"

"Father thinks it's dangerous." She sighed. She might as well tell him everything. "And it's a punishment for talking back."

Charlie chuckled. "Well, that's something you and Carrie share. Her mouth was always getting her in trouble." He frowned. "But I don't remember your father keeping her from the woods. He couldn't . . . she would have gone anyway."

Francie sucked in her breath. "Well, I'm not Carrie," she said. Carrie hadn't had to look at her parents' sad faces or feel the guilt whenever she disobeyed them. It happened often enough, anyway. She saw a flicker of something flash in Charlie's eyes and as quickly disappear. He was disappointed in her, she thought, fighting against that lump that always formed in her throat when people compared her to her sister.

But Charlie only nodded. "It's different now," he said. The logging whistle screamed, shattering the peace of the quiet street and calling the men to work. He touched her shoulder with one finger. "I'll get the message. And I'll come see you on Sunday. After all, if she's haunting you, there must be a reason." He grinned at her. "Carrie always had a reason." He settled his hat down low on his forehead and ran off toward the lumberyard.

Francie stared after him. He'd been joking, she knew that. But somehow the words hung in the air. "Carrie always had a reason," she whispered.

· Chapter Four ·

"Charlie's back." Francie let the back door shut as she came into the warm kitchen. "He's going to be chute rider again. And he's still joking about how he'll ride the flume this year."

Her mother looked up from the oatmeal she was stirring at the big black cookstove. "That boy always was crazy," she answered, shaking her head. "I'll have to give him a talking to." Charlie's father and Francie's mother were brother and sister, and when he was younger, Charlie spent every summer up in the mountains. He used to stay with the Cavanaughs, but after Carrie died he stopped coming. Then, two years ago he hired on with the lumber company as a logger.

"What were you doing out so early?" Francie's mother frowned at her.

Francie hesitated, wanting to tell the truth. But somehow it just wouldn't come. "I . . . I woke up early and it smelled so clean and new outside . . ." That was part of the truth, anyway. "I just had to get out in it."

Her mother smiled. "Summer in the mountains. There's nothing like it, is there?" She glanced out the window framed with yellow checked curtains. "If we only had the time to enjoy it more."

Francie took a breath and plunged in. "Don't you think Father would let me go to the basin, just until I finish counting the tree rings for Mr. Court?" And figure out about Carrie's message, she added silently.

Her mother's hand paused in its stirring. Francie knew she believed promises were important.

"Don't you see, child?" Her mother turned to look at her. "If Mr. Court has his way, he'd stop the logging altogether. The loggers would leave. The town would die. We'd have to close the hotel, and this hotel is your father's life." She turned back to the oatmeal. "Please set the table now. Breakfast will soon be ready."

Francie began laying the silver and china on the dining room table as her father came into the dining room with the *St. Joseph Herald* under his arm. Mr. Court's paper. "Good morning, Frances," he said as he pulled out his chair and sat down.

"Good morning, Father," she answered, wishing he would at least smile at her. But it would do no good to be sulky. It would only anger him more. She watched as he unfolded the paper, shook it out, and began to read. Francie had always been proud of her tall, handsome father. She loved the way he brushed his thick dark hair back from his forehead. His mustache was neatly combed and waxed, and the creases in his suit pants were so sharp it seemed you could cut your finger on them. His one vanity, as he always put it, was his bright-colored waistcoats. The one he wore today had a red-and-black-plaid pattern. Francie knew his friends teased him about his waistcoats—he only laughed and wore them anyway. She sighed silently. He could laugh with his friends, but not with his family. Not anymore.

Francie sat down in her place and folded her hands in her lap. What could she say to make him change his mind and give her permission to go to the basin? The headlines on the front page of the paper caught her eye. DEPRESSION WORSENS, they screamed. She wondered if that bad news would make it harder or easier to talk to him.

Now's the time, her mind was humming. Ask him now. A lump was forming in her throat, blocking her speech. "Father, I . . ." She swallowed again. "I'm sorry for what I said last night."

He looked at her over the top of his paper and gave a short nod. "I should hope so."

"But, Father." She stretched her hand out, almost touching his arm. "I promised Mr. Court I'd count the tree rings for him. I don't want to break my promise."

"It's a promise you should never have made," her father said. There was no anger there; his voice had the same flat tone as always. "You'll just have to tell Mr. Court you're unable to fulfill your obligations. I'm sure he can get someone else to help."

"But that's just the point, Father," Francie countered. "You can't stop him from finding out how old the tree was, so I might as well get to keep my promise." Her father smoothed down his mustache with one finger, and Francie took it as a sign that he was listening. "Could I just go to the basin until I finish counting the tree rings? Then I promise I'll never go back."

"You know I don't hold with what Court is doing," her father said at last. "He's standing in the way of human progress."

Francie took a breath. Was he wavering? She crossed her fingers under the table.

Her father sighed. "Well, I'm glad to see you're taking your promises seriously," he said. He frowned at her. "I don't say it's safe . . ."

"I'll be very careful," Francie said. "I won't go anywhere near the logging."

Francie's mother came into the dining room with oatmeal in a pottery dish. She placed it in front of Francie's father, who plopped a steaming spoonful of the cereal in Francie's bowl. "Only until you've finished counting the rings." He served Francie's mother and then himself. "At

least Court can't accuse me of choosing sides," he muttered.

Francie sang as she helped Josie change the sheets in the
hotel rooms. But by the time she'd finished that and
helped her mother make raspberry tarts for the hotel
guests' dinners, washed up all the dirty breakfast dishes
and then the dinner dishes, it was late afternoon. "It's not
fair," she mumbled, hanging the wet dishrag on its rack by
the sink. "They tell me I can go to the basin and then keep
me so busy there's no time."

"Did you say something, Francie?" Her mother pumped
a last stream of water from the small hand pump on the
counter to rinse the dishpan clean of suds. The hotel
boasted the latest in modern conveniences—there was
even a drain connecting the dry sink to a pipe that ran
under the hotel and emptied the sink water out away from
the buildings.

"No, ma'am." Francie turned away so her mother
couldn't see her face. "When do we need to begin supper?"

Her mother dried her hands on her apron. "Oh, not for
a while, and I can get it started." She pulled a pin out of
her hair and repositioned it. "I've got some paperwork to
finish now." She was on her way out of the hotel kitchen,
and then turned around. "Do you need something to do?"

Francie glanced up to see her eyes twinkling. "No,
ma'am," she answered, grinning. "I can find something to

occupy myself." She followed her mother out of the kitchen, down the hall, and into the lobby of the hotel. Father always said their lobby was as elegant as any in New York City. A large Oriental carpet covered the floor, and chairs and tables, mostly in the French Victorian style, were arranged conveniently for guests to converse with one another. A glittering crystal chandelier hung from the high ceiling. The windows looking out onto the street had carved panes of leaded glass. Her father and Mr. Morgan, one of the regular guests, were sitting in wing-back chairs in the corner of the room. Their teacups were forgotten on the small round table between them while they talked intensely about something. "Probably the depression," Francie muttered. It was the only thing anyone talked about these days. She walked around the perimeter of the room rather than straight across to the front door, making sure her father's back was toward her.

She opened the heavy doors with their leaded glass inserts, slipped outside, and closed them again without a sound, breathing a sigh of relief. She glanced down—her mother might not want her traipsing through the woods in her new shoes, but there wasn't time to change now. She turned, and skirting around the buildings, she climbed the hill behind the hotel and headed off to Connor's Basin.

• Chapter Five •

It was a half-hour walk to the stump where Carrie's message was hidden. The road ran along the edge of the basin, and Francie's shoes were covered with dust by the time she'd reached the footpath that led down into the shallow valley where the biggest sequoias once stood. Birds flew out of the grass as she passed, and squirrels scampered up the huge gray stumps that towered over her head.

Small seedlings of sugar and yellow pine and even tiny sequoias were springing up in the turf. Francie bent down to smooth away the grass threatening to overwhelm one small sprout that reached stubbornly for the sun, and as she did, an image of her sister flashed into her mind. Carrie, pushing back the grass in just this way. "This one's a sugar pine, Francie," she was saying, "and here's a baby sequoia. Can you believe they grow so big?" Francie stood up, shaking her head to rid herself of the memory. Was there any place not stamped with Carrie's presence?

She marched quickly along the path. Surely not here, she thought, not where Carrie had wandered every day of her life. She looked around at the huge stumps and shattered trunks and wondered what Carrie would have thought of this graveyard of giants. It looked like a battlefield, she thought sadly. A battlefield with half the soldiers lying still unburied.

She reached her stump, the beginning of all the carnage, and set the rickety ladder upright. She climbed up to the hole, carefully avoiding the broken rung, and extracted the oilskin bag. Then she pulled herself to the top of the stump and sat down with her feet dangling over the edge. A squirrel chattered at her from a nearby stump and she threw a pebble at him. "Oh, be quiet," she said. "You sound just like Father!" The squirrel ignored the pebble, which had come nowhere near him, and kept up his unintelligible commentary.

Francie pulled the note out of the bag. The paper was yellow, and the creases were black where it had lain folded so long.

> Meet me at Turkey Fork
> half past four on Sunday.
> Don't tell anyone—the only safety is in secrecy.

• • •

What could it mean? Francie turned the paper over, but the other side was blank. She felt like screaming. How could she ever find out? It was impossible.

She sighed, put the paper back in the bag, and slipped it into her pocket. Then she pulled out her hair comb. She pulled her hair back to keep it out of her eyes and fastened it with the comb and a few pins. Here, where there was no one to see, it didn't matter how much she looked like her sister.

She crawled over to the mark she'd made on the 2,500th ring. She put her finger on the next ring and began to count, touching each ring carefully with the tip of her fingernail. "Five hundred and one. Five hundred and two. Five hundred and three . . ." Soon the squirrel lost interest and disappeared over the edge of the stump. The birds went back to their songs, and the basin settled into a familiar late afternoon quiet.

"What are you doing up there, girl?"

The voice startled Francie so much her hand jerked off the 2,727th ring. She sat up, heart pounding, and looked around. Coming down the path was Lewis Granger, the manager of the lumber company.

Francie glanced quickly back at the tree rings, realizing that she'd lost her place. Thank goodness she made a mark every hundred rings—she'd only have to count twenty-seven rings over again. "Hello, Mr. Granger," she called, sitting up.

The man paused. His balding head gleamed in the sun, and his eyes, glinting behind his wire-rimmed glasses, looked speculative.

Francie stood up quickly and came to the edge of the stump. There was something in his manner that made her nervous.

Mr. Granger stared at her without speaking. Finally he grunted. "What are you doing on that stump? How did you get up there?"

This was the man who was in charge of all the lumbering in this part of the mountains. He wouldn't be very happy to hear that Frank Court was launching a campaign to stop the logging. "I climbed that," she said, indicating the old ladder. "I'm just enjoying the view." She crossed her fingers behind her back. She was enjoying the view— that was the truth.

Mr. Granger came to the bottom of the ladder. Most of the other loggers wore rough pants and flannel shirts, but Lewis Granger always wore a suit, though it was wrinkled and baggy—as if he'd slept in his clothes. His muscled arms were long in proportion to his body, reminding Francie of an ape—a short, balding ape with a fat belly. He smiled at her, squinting, blocking the sun with one hand. "This property belongs to the lumber company."

Francie hesitated. "My father gave me permission to come," she said at last. "He knows I'm here." Hopefully that was truth, she thought. Mama had no doubt told him.

His smiled broadened. "Your father owns the hotel," he said, "not the lumber company." He put his hand on the ladder. "This is private property."

Francie could feel her heart start beating faster. Was he going to climb the ladder? If he was angry because she was trespassing, why was he smiling? She put her hand in her pocket and felt the little bag with Carrie's note. Closing her hand over it, she looked down at him. "We often come here for picnics," she said. That wasn't strictly true: Other people had picnics here, the Cavanaughs stopped having picnics when Carrie died. But Mr. Granger wouldn't know that, would he?

"People break the law all the time," he said. He put one foot on the lowest rung of the ladder. "It's only a problem if they get caught." The sun flashed on his glasses, making his eyes invisible.

Francie looked at his hands on the ladder and suddenly remembered how the rung had broken under her weight yesterday. Would the ladder hold him if he tried to climb? Should she warn him? If it broke under him, he'd be madder than ever. She had taken a breath to tell him the ladder wasn't safe, when she heard someone running down the path.

"Francie!" She looked up. It was Charlie, coming to get the note. "What are you doing here?"

As soon as he heard Charlie's voice, Mr. Granger stepped away from the ladder. He brushed off his hands and pulled out his pocket watch to check the time. "Meeting your sweetheart?" he said softly. "Did your father give you permission to do that, too?"

Francie stared down at the man, confused and suddenly angry. "Charlie's my cousin!" she retorted.

Charlie came around the tree stump and stopped, his smile fading when he saw Mr. Granger. "Afternoon," he said, nodding.

"Good afternoon, Charlie," Mr. Granger said. "Nice evening for a walk."

"Yes, sir." Charlie shoved his hands into his pockets. He looked up at Francie. "I didn't know you'd be here, cuz," he said to her. "I thought . . ." He glanced at Mr. Granger. "I thought you had to work at the hotel."

"Father said I could have some time off," she said, watching Mr. Granger.

The man's eyes flickered behind his glasses. "Well, I'll leave you two young people to your fun." He smiled up at Francie again, turned, and walked back along the path to the road.

Charlie followed him around the stump and he and Francie waited in silence until the man disappeared over the top of the rise.

"What was he doing here?" Charlie frowned up at Francie. He must have come straight here after work. His clothes were filthy, his face was streaked with dirt, and dried blood marked a scratch on one cheek, probably from a low-hanging limb. Charlie's job was to ride on top of the long chain of logs as they were dragged down the logging chute from the woods to the mill, and if his only injuries were scratches he was lucky.

"I don't know. Are you coming up?" She patted a place beside her on the stump.

Charlie took one look at the ladder and shook his head. "That would never hold me," he said. "It might be the same one Carrie and I used to reach the hole, but I'm a lot bigger now and it's a lot older. You come down, and I'll catch you if it breaks. Did you get Carrie's note?"

"I've got it," Francie said, climbing down. She tested each rung of the ladder before she put her weight on it. When she was standing on the ground, she handed Charlie the bag.

He took it, smoothing the cloth with his fingers. He turned it over several times, and then cleared his throat. "Yep. We used to put messages in here." He looked at Francie and blinked. "Would you do me a favor?"

"Sure." Francie smiled at him.

"Take that comb out of your hair." He looked away. "With your hair up like that you look so much like her I feel like I'm the one she's haunting." Then he laughed. "Do you mind?"

Francie shook her head and unpinned her hair. "No,"

she said, sighing. "I just wish . . ." She turned to him. "Are we trespassing?"

"What?" Charlie stared at her. "Now?"

"The lumber company owns this land," Francie said. "Is it against the law for us to be here? Mr. Granger said it was."

"Did he?" Charlie looked back toward the path. "I guess it is private land," he said. "Lots of people come here, but nobody's made a stink about it before. Is that why Granger was here?"

Francie shrugged. "Maybe he really was just out for a walk." She leaned up against the ladder, and then turned to look at it. "I thought he was going to climb up—he was just starting to when you came."

Charlie shook his head. "He weighs more than I do. All he'd have to do is look at that ladder to know it would break under him."

Francie looked at him. "Then he was trying to make me think he was going to come up. Why?" She shuddered. "It was kind of scary. I didn't know what he was going to do—push me off the stump? He just kept smiling."

Charlie grunted. "Granger's a mean one. He likes to scare people he thinks are weaker than he is." His eyes twinkled. "What he doesn't know is that you could have climbed down and been miles away before he'd even run a few steps. I'll bet you're still the fastest runner around here."

Francie bit her lip. "I haven't had much occasion to run lately."

Charlie nodded, seeming to understand. "I thought you weren't allowed out here anymore."

Francie grinned. "I talked Father into a slight reprieve." She explained about Mr. Court wanting her to count the tree rings.

"That might take quite awhile," he said. He gave her a wink. "And I think he wants you to count some of the others as well, doesn't he?"

"We'll see how long it takes to count one," she answered, trying to look serious. She took the bag, extracted the note, and handed it to him. "What do you think it means?"

Charlie puzzled over the words. "Well," he said, "I know where Turkey Fork is." He pushed his hat back and scratched his head. "At least I used to know. Your sister made up the name—we saw a turkey there once, though you hardly ever see them in the mountains. It was on Connor's Creek, where the streambed branched." He rubbed his chin, thinking. "Or was it Dead Man's Creek?" He shrugged. "I can't remember, Francie." He looked at the paper again. "It's her handwriting, though. I'm sure of that."

"Do you think you'd recognize Turkey Fork if you got there?" Francie touched his arm. "Could we just walk along the creek till we found it?"

"Not if it was Dead Man's Creek," Charlie answered, "that one's all dried up. Hasn't had water running in it since they dammed the river. But if it was Connor's Creek, maybe we could." He looked at the sun, riding just above the top of the farther ridge. "It'll be dark soon. What about Sunday afternoon? It's supposed to be a nice day, and it probably wouldn't take us more than two hours to walk the lower part of Connor up to the first fork and back." He handed her back the note. "What do you think we'll find?"

"I don't have any idea," Francie said, surprised that he would give up his Sunday afternoon to go searching the woods with her. The fact that he actually seemed interested made her nervous. What if it was nothing? He'd think she was being silly.

Charlie shrugged. "Probably nothing," he said as if he'd read her thoughts. "Your sister was a great one for secrets." He tugged on the brim of his hat, pulling it down on his forehead. It made him look older, more serious. "Mostly they were little secrets, like the time she found a den of fox pups." He touched the bag in Francie's hand. "But somehow I feel like we owe it to her to try to find out what this one was. It's kind of like a message from beyond the grave."

Francie suddenly remembered her dream, and she shivered. "You don't really believe that, do you?"

Charlie shook his head. "No, I don't. Not really." Francie thought his voice sounded almost regretful. "But

I'd like to know what she meant, wouldn't you?"

"We'll probably never find out." Suddenly impatient, she turned her back on him and started walking up the path. "Come on . . . if I don't get home in time to help Mama, I won't be allowed to come back."

Charlie ran to catch up with her. "What about her diary? She might have written something about it. Did you check her diary?"

Francie spun around so fast she nearly ran into him. "What diary?"

Charlie caught her arm and kept them both from falling in a heap. "Carrie's diary. It had a dark blue leather binding and gold letters. She used to bring it out here and write something almost every day—all about animals and plants and things. You can't have forgotten that!"

But she had forgotten. Francie stared at him, but instead she saw Carrie, sitting on a fallen log, chewing at the end of her pencil and staring off into space. On her lap was the diary. "Yes," she whispered, "I remember now." How could she have forgotten? She had always longed to write, too, even before she knew how, but Carrie would only let her touch the soft leather cover . . . sometimes. "What do you suppose happened to it?"

Charlie shrugged. "You didn't find it after . . ." he began, and then swallowed. "It wasn't with her things?"

Francie felt the lump rise in her own throat. "They

wouldn't even go into her room for a long time." She remembered that—how she had felt compelled to tiptoe past, as if her sister was sleeping eternally behind that closed door. "Finally Mama did have all her clothes washed and ironed. Then she gave them to the poor." That was another thing she remembered, Carrie's dresses hanging out on the line to dry. Mama and Mrs. Parker did it all in one day when Father was gone to St. Joseph. "They must have gone through her things, eventually, because Mama asked me if I wanted her locket. But I never saw her diary, and I forgot all about it."

Charlie rubbed his chin. "I think she kept it hidden," he said slowly. "She always said it was to keep you from prying into her things." He put his hand on Francie's shoulder almost in apology. "But it was really because she loved secrets. She knew you'd never have read it without asking."

Francie felt her face go hot, but when she saw the sorrow stamped on Charlie's handsome face, the angry words died on her lips. She sighed, instead. "I never could understand her," she said. "And she never did understand me, either." Her eyes stung with unshed tears, and she turned away. "I've got to get back. It's getting dark. Father will be worried."

Charlie tugged again on his hat brim. "I'll walk back with you," he said. "Uncle James knows I'd not let anything happen to you."

Francie nodded. It was true. Father had let Carrie wander the mountains alone even in the dark, but Francie always had to have someone to take care of her. She gritted her teeth to keep from saying so out loud and followed her cousin back to town.

· Chapter Six ·

It was late when Francie finally finished helping her mother in the kitchen and was allowed to go upstairs to her room. She didn't tiptoe past Carrie's door anymore, but out of habit she always walked quietly. She had her hand on the doorknob of her own room when she suddenly made up her mind. Turning back, she put her hand on Carrie's doorknob. Would the door be locked? Her heart began to beat faster. Nobody had ever said she couldn't go into her sister's room, but she had never done so before. For six years the door had stood firmly closed.

Francie knew that sometimes her mother went in. Once in a very great while she heard faint crying from behind the door. It was never mentioned, and somehow Francie knew her mother would not appreciate her acknowledging it.

Now Francie turned the knob. It clicked, and with a little push the door swung open. With a quick glance over her shoulder to be sure nobody was coming up the stairs, Francie stepped into her sister's room and shut the door behind her.

Francie stood with her back against the door, waiting until her eyes got used to the darkness. The air was still and smelled musty. "They never open the windows," Francie mumbled. She felt her way to Carrie's bed—her furniture matched Francie's own, and the room was a mirror image of Francie's—and sat down. Her hands found the small nightstand and the oil lamp on it. Inside the drawer Francie found matches. She lit one and held the flame up to examine the lamp. "Surely there won't be oil in it," she said aloud, but she was wrong. The lamp was full of oil, and the glass chimney was shining—as if someone had just cleaned it recently. She touched the match to the wick, then quickly turned the flame down low. The drapes were pulled tightly closed, but Francie wasn't taking any chances. She didn't want to have to explain her presence here.

The room didn't quite look as if nobody lived in it—the bed with its plump pillows was covered with a thin comforter, although Francie could feel that there weren't any blankets or sheets under it—just the stiff ticking of the feather bed. The dresser had a crocheted scarf spread out on top, several colored bottles, and another lamp. The wardrobe door was closed, but Francie knew if she opened it she would find it empty. She ran her hand over the smooth wood of the nightstand and then looked at the tip of her finger in the lamplight—no dust. Someone cleaned in here, then.

But it certainly didn't look like Carrie lived here. When Carrie was alive, her room had almost exploded in a kind of cheerful chaos. Clothes were thrown over chairs and the bed spindles or dropped on the floor in a heap. Old birds' nests graced all the windowsills, and pinecones balanced in a line on the top of the wainscoting. Rocks glittering with strains of quartz and mica were piled on the dresser, and feathers bristled out in all directions from behind the mirror. Carrie's bookcase was always half empty because she left the books stacked on the floor with flowers and leaves pressed between the pages.

Now the books were lined up neatly on the shelves of the bookcase. Francie ran her finger across their spines. There were books about plants, animals, and geology. There was poetry . . . Whitman and Wordsworth were Carrie's favorites. There was a huge dictionary. But there was no diary that Francie could see.

She opened all the drawers in the dresser—they were empty. She already knew it wasn't in the nightstand drawer—it had contained nothing but the box of matches.

Charlie had said that Carrie had kept the diary hidden. Francie stood in the middle of the room and turned around in a slow circle. She wondered suddenly if Carrie herself had stood here long ago and looked around her room for a hiding place. "If I were Carrie, where would I hide my diary?" Francie whispered. She thought about how Charlie had said Carrie loved mysteries. Then it wouldn't have been in the drawers, even buried under her clothes—that would be too easy. Wouldn't Carrie have picked a more mysterious spot?

Under the feather bed? She touched it with a finger. No, that wouldn't work—Mama and Josie turned the mattresses every month and put them out in the sun twice a year to air out. Anything hidden under there would be found.

Her glance fell on the wardrobe. "Maybe it has a secret compartment," Francie murmured, and as soon as she'd said the words, she knew that's what Carrie would have loved—a secret compartment. The two narrow doors of the wardrobe met in the center. Francie walked over and opened them. As she had expected, it was empty. She ran her hand along the side panels and the back. The wood was thin and hid no secrets.

She knocked on the bottom of the cabinet, producing a muffled thud. Shouldn't it sound more hollow? Her heart started hammering in her chest. Kneeling, she reached under the wardrobe and placed her other hand on the outside of the wood. Then she knocked again. It still sounded muffled, and she couldn't feel any vibration.

"It's got a false bottom!" Almost frantic, she ran her fingers over the floor of the wardrobe. It felt smooth, but on the right side there was a slight indentation—a nick in the wood as if someone had dropped something heavy and it had made a mark. No one would pay the least attention to it—unless she were thinking about secret compartments. Francie turned her finger over, dug her nail into the nick, and pulled up.

It moved! Francie's heart was beating so hard she thought she might faint. She lifted the board and looked underneath. In the dim light from the oil lamp, she could see a book lying in the space between the true bottom of the wardrobe and the false bottom installed above it. Francie reached in and her hand closed on the soft, smooth leather. The diary! She lifted it out, placed it on the floor beside her, and then lowered the board, tapping it back into place with her knuckles. She felt the smooth wood with her fingers. How had Carrie made this secret place? Or had she just happened to discover that her wardrobe had a false bottom? "I'll never know," Francie murmured, but it crossed her mind to check her own wardrobe. Maybe it had a secret compartment as well!

A creaking step outside in the hallway had her leaping to her feet. She spun around, staring at the door. She had absolutely no idea how long she'd been in Carrie's room. She listened as the steps moved slowly down the hall and into her parents' room—it must be her father heading for bed. Mama would be coming soon, and she often stopped in Francie's room for a final good night.

Francie grabbed the book, shut the wardrobe doors as quietly as she could, and blew out the lamp. She walked on tiptoe to the door. No sound came from the hallway. Slowly she turned the knob and cracked the door ever so slightly. She held her breath. She could hear the rustle of her mother's dress as she moved around downstairs in the parlor. Quickly Francie slipped out the door, shut it silently, took three steps to her own door, opened it, and slipped inside.

For the second time that night Francie stood in the middle of a room and waited until her eyes grew accustomed to the dark and her fast-beating heart stilled to normal. There were no sounds of footsteps in the hall. After a moment she moved to her nightstand and lit the lamp. She clutched Carrie's diary to her chest and looked around the room. She must find a place to hide it here, quickly, before her mother knocked on her door.

Without much hope, she threw open the doors of her own wardrobe. She felt the floor, but though it was the twin of Carrie's in every other way, she could tell immediately that there was no false bottom—instead, the true bottom of the cabinet dropped two inches below the level of the door opening. "Maybe Carrie's false bottom would fit here," she said, and knew as she said it that she was right. If she could somehow sneak the board from Carrie's room to her own, it would slide easily into the floor of her wardrobe and rest smoothly at the level of the door opening. Maybe tomorrow she could try that, but there was no time tonight.

She heard a slight pop as her mother put her feet on the first step. Jumping up, Francie looked around the room. She could hide the book in the dresser, under her clothes, but sometimes her mother opened Francie's drawers, putting away mended clothes, and looking for tears to have Josie repair. It was too risky.

Creaks from the hallway told Francie that her mother was at the top of the stairs and moving down the hallway. Francie looked up. Her wardrobe had a kind of crown of carved wood around the top, and just as her mother knocked on her door, Francie put her foot on the edge of the wardrobe floor, boosted herself up, and dropped the diary down behind the carved panel. It was only a temporary solution, she knew, because Josie dusted up there regularly, but for tonight it would do. It wasn't likely that her mother would want to check the top of the wardrobe tonight.

"Francie?" her mother's soft voice came through the door. "Are you still awake?"

Francie dropped down onto the overstuffed chair in the corner, grabbed a random book from her bookshelf, and drew a breath to answer. "Yes, Mama. Please come in." She was surprised to find that her voice sounded firm. It was only her hands that were trembling.

"You're not even ready for bed yet!" The surprise showed in her mother's voice, as she came in carrying a set of Francie's underdrawers. "Is everything all right?" She went to Francie's dresser, opened it, and laid the underdrawers on the top of the pile.

Francie felt her face going hot and was grateful for the lamp's low light. "I'm fine, Mama," she said. "I just got involved in my reading." She smoothed her hand over the cover of the book in her lap.

"Are there any other clothes to mend?"

Francie watched her mother finger through the piles of clothes in her drawer and thanked the impulse that made her look elsewhere for a hiding place. "I don't think so."

Her mother looked at the book, and Francie knew her next question would be what she was reading. She must change the subject.

"I wanted . . ." Her mind churned. "I wanted to thank you for talking to Father," she rattled on. "He's allowing me to go to Connor's Basin after all."

"I didn't talk to him," her mother said. "You are quite persistent enough on your own." She smiled. "But he does believe in keeping promises. He's quite pleased that you feel the same."

Francie swallowed, feeling guilt sweep over her. She was deceiving her father. How could she do such a thing? But how could she not find out about Carrie's note and her diary?

"I do," she said, vowing that after this she would never deceive her parents again. Or break a promise.

Her mother rose. "I hope you'll go to sleep soon," she said. "It's not good for your eyes to be reading in this low light."

Francie nodded. "I'm done for tonight," she said. She rose, kissed her mother good night, and shut the door after her. Then she picked up the book she'd pulled off the shelf—*An Essay Concerning Human Understanding*.

Francie almost laughed out loud. Would her mother have believed she was sitting up late reading a philosophy book? Not likely!

· Chapter Seven ·

May 7, 1886. A robin is sitting on a branch directly above my head as I write this—if I had a worm he might come eat out of my hand! It's so warm today—I will take off my shoes and stockings and go wading in Dead Man's Creek, even though the water temperature is not far above freezing. Tomorrow I will take the trail that leads up to Connor's Peak. The weather promises to be fine, and I hope to make the summit before midday.

May 8, 1886. I did it! I hiked all the way up to Connor's Peak and back again. Papa was furious, for I didn't make it home before dark and missed supper. He is terrified that something terrible will happen to me—that I'll be eaten by a bear. Silly—as if I didn't know to make noise and scare the bears off! As punishment I was not allowed to eat at all, but I don't care. The view from the top was food enough for me.

The snowcapped peaks beyond were wreathed in clouds and seemed to touch the blue, blue sky—the smell of pine resin was heady perfume. The delicate mountain violets are just beginning to bloom—I think they are my favorite of the wildflowers. Charlie will be so jealous that I went without him, but I wanted to be absolutely alone at the summit. Does God feel like that sometimes—wishing He could be all alone with His creations, without the pesky humans crawling all over the place like stinging ants?

Francie scowled. It was like Carrie to compare herself with God. Her handwriting was scrawling and spidery—Francie remembered their mother always pointing out how illegible Carrie's school papers were. Francie ran her thumb along the gilt edges of the little book—the pages were soft, almost like cloth. A part of her wanted to read through the night, and a part of her didn't want to read it at all. It felt wrong, somehow—as if she were peering into someone's bedroom window and watching the most private part of that person's life. Suddenly she wanted to slam the book shut and hurl it across the room. Why did Carrie have to be so incredibly stupid as to get caught in a landslide!

But stronger than her reluctance and anger was the compulsion to find out about the note and what mystery surrounded it. She felt as if she couldn't quite catch her breath as she turned to the last page. It was dated Aug. 13, 1888, two days before the landslide. Carrie's handwriting was even more scrawly than usual, with several ink blots, which seemed to indicate either that she was in a great hurry or that she was very upset.

Aug. 13, 1888. I saw Old Robert again today. He took me up over the mountain and showed me my tree. My tree! It is enormous, bigger than any other sequoia in the entire valley. Maybe it's the biggest tree in the entire world! And so old . . . think of the history it has witnessed. I can't fathom it. It is so, so beautiful . . . a Prince among trees. No, a King . . . an Emperor! And I am the steward. No, I am the knight, sworn to protect my Emperor or die in the attempt! Can Old Robert really give me a tree? He says he can . . . he showed me the will and it looks very official. He says I must not tell anyone about this great gift. But how can I keep silent? I am bursting with the joy and the responsibility. I will tell Charlie—he can keep the secret. And perhaps I should consult with someone who knows about wills. Surely it would be safe to tell Mr. Court. As soon as I can find a way into St. Joseph, I will make an appointment to see him. After the White Mountain walking tour—they're counting on me to be there for that.

Francie shut the book with a sharp *pop*. The White Mountain walking tour. Before the landslide it used to be offered every year for the tourists. People from St. Joseph and from even farther away would come to see the wild-flowers, the sequoias, the deep canyons cut by the river, and the powerful river itself—all the views the Sierras were becoming famous for. Carrie had been allowed to go as a sort of assistant guide, to help the ladies over the rougher parts of the trail.

They'd brought her sister's body back—Francie had watched as they'd lifted her off the mule. She could remember the feeling of the splintery hitching post—she'd stood beside the mule, rubbing and rubbing that post with her fingers as she'd listened to the story of what had happened.

"Mrs. Jenkins spied a clump of that yellow columbine way out on one of them rock outcroppings," the old guide had said. "I told her it was too dangerous, but she wouldn't let it rest, she begged Carrie to climb out and get it for her." The old man rubbed a shaky hand over his chin and pulled his hat brim down lower over his eyes. Francie, looking up at him, could see the tears running down his grizzled cheeks. "That silly woman kept pestering her—talking as if Carrie was afeared to try it," he said through clenched teeth. "I think Carrie tried it just to shut her up. She started out and the whole thing collapsed." He closed his eyes, as if by doing that he could erase the picture in his mind. "It was only luck we found her body—she was more than half covered with that broken rock."

It had been the last of the White Mountain walking tours. No guide had dared to advertise anything so dangerous in the six years since. The tourists still came, but they didn't go up on White Mountain anymore. Carrie was buried in the mountains she had loved. And, thought Francie, smoothing the soft leather of the diary with her finger, her secrets were buried with her.

Who was Old Robert? Where was this tree he had supposedly given her? Francie opened the diary once more and looked at the pages. Could she find more clues to this mystery in the diary? It would mean reading the entire book, entry by entry. She closed her eyes. How could she bear to read her sister's most private thoughts?

"I must bear it," she whispered. "For the sake of Carrie's mystery." She smiled a bitter little half smile. While she was alive, Carrie was always inventing pretend mysteries. But when she died, she set off a real mystery. How she would have loved to solve it!

She heard her father's footsteps walk past the door and then stop. Francie blew out the lamp before her father could knock on her door—no more time now to search. And she wouldn't see Charlie again until Sunday—if he remembered to come.

On Sunday afternoon Charlie knocked on the Cavanaughs' door just as he had promised. Francie moved to open it, but her mother motioned her to sit and went to answer it herself.

"Aunt Mary," Charlie said, taking off his hat as he stepped into the front hallway.

"Come in, Charlie." Francie's mother gave him a hug and showed him into the sitting room where Francie and her father were waiting. "Sit down and tell us the news." She picked up her knitting and sat down in her favorite green brocade chair. When she was a little girl, Francie had loved to sneak into the sitting room and run her fingers through the slippery gold tassels that hung from the seat cushions.

"Yes, ma'am." Charlie took a seat beside Francie on the sofa. He smiled at her, raising one eyebrow in question.

Francie nodded her head ever so slightly. She felt like she might burst with the news of the diary, but instead she had to sit quietly with her hands folded in her lap while her mother and father questioned Charlie about his family and friends from St. Joseph.

"Old Mrs. Andrew died just after New Year's," Charlie was saying.

Francie's father put down his newspaper and stared at him. "I wonder if that was the same Mrs. Andrew who taught me in school."

"Probably was," Charlie said. "They said she was eighty-six. She came west in the 1850s and she was in her forties then!"

"I'm amazed she didn't die long ago," Francie's father said, "with the things she had to put up with from her students. She used to tell us we were more of a challenge than the Oregon Trail." He smiled at the memory, and Francie felt her heart twist inside her. If only he would smile more often.

She was torn between wanting her father to tell more stories and wanting to go with Charlie to Turkey Fork. Her father had been eight and her mother only a year younger when their families came west, and their wagon train experiences were exciting—she remembered some of the stories she'd heard when she was little. Before Carrie died.

But the light in her father's eyes dimmed as quickly as it had come. There would be no more stories now. Francie sighed and surreptitiously poked Charlie.

"Uncle James," he said, sitting up straight. "I was wondering if I could take Francie walking up the Connor's Creek trail. The bluebirds are thick up in there . . . and I think I know where a den of fox pups is. We were talking the other day and she said she'd like to see them."

"I would, Father," Francie said, gritting her teeth against the tone Charlie was using, like she was a little girl who had to be taken care of. The point, she told herself sternly, was to find Turkey Fork. "Please may I go? We'll be home before dark."

Her father looked from Charlie to Francie, and then at Francie's mother, who took that moment to examine her knitting. He cleared his throat but evidently decided there was no trick. "I suppose you may go," he said, nodding. He fixed Francie with a stern look. "No climbing or doing anything dangerous. You will obey Charlie. Do you understand?"

"Yes, Father." Francie gripped the brocaded arm of the sofa to keep herself from jumping up.

He nodded once more. Charlie put his hand on Francie's elbow as if he were helping her to rise. "I'll take care of her," he said, turning back to Francie's parents as Francie almost skipped into the hall, grabbed her hat from the rack, and fixed it on her head with a few pins. She hated hats—their wide brims limited what she could see without craning her neck—but she knew her mother would never let her go walking with Charlie without one. As quietly as she could, she opened the middle drawer of the hall table and pulled out an old cotton shoulder bag with Carrie's diary inside. She'd put it there that morning, sneaking down the stairs with it before anyone else was awake.

"Yes, sir," Charlie was saying. "No risks. I promise." He stepped into the dim hallway, opened the front door, and ushered Francie out into the street.

· Chapter Eight ·

Francie took a deep breath of the pine-scented air. "Carrie was right," she said, looking at Charlie. "The smell of the air in the mountains is almost better than food!"

Charlie raised his eyebrows. "Well, I wouldn't go that far," he said, grinning. "How do you know what Carrie said? Has she been talking to you now?"

Francie frowned at him. She reached into the bag, which she'd slung over her shoulder, and held out the diary. "I found it. There was a secret compartment in her wardrobe." She stroked the book's soft blue binding. "Now there's a secret compartment in my wardrobe," she whispered.

Charlie stopped walking. He looked down at the book in Francie's hand, but he didn't take it—and the expression on his face looked as if he thought it might be as dangerous as a rattlesnake. "Did you read it?" He looked up at Francie, but still he didn't take the diary.

"Parts of it," she answered. She touched Charlie's elbow and he started forward. "How far up Connor's Creek will we have to go, do you think?"

He shrugged and gave her sideways glance. "Did you find anything about . . . you know, the secret?"

As an answer, Francie opened the diary to the last entry and read it aloud as they walked. She left out the date and the part about the White Mountain walking tour.

"This tree," Francie put her finger on the diary page when she'd finished reading. "Maybe it's the secret Carrie was talking about in the note. Can we find it?"

Charlie looked down at her. "Don't you think it's been cut by now? If it's as big as she says . . ." He didn't need to finish the thought.

Francie closed her eyes. "You're probably right," she said. "Do you know this man, Old Robert?"

"Old Robert." Charlie stroked his chin and smoothed his mustache away from his mouth. "He's that old hermit who used to live up near Connor's Pass—Carrie took me to his cabin once. He hasn't been around here in a long time."

"Connor's Pass—that's just below Connor's Peak." Francie's heart gave a little jump. Connor's Peak was the mountain Carrie had mentioned climbing, and, suddenly, Francie wanted to climb it as well, to see the view that

Carrie had described in her diary. "Let's head up that way." She tucked the diary back into the shoulder bag.

Charlie scratched his head. "I promised I'd get you back before dark."

"You did not!" Francie turned on him. "You just said you'd take care of me. And besides, that was just so Father would let me go. I can take care of myself."

"Yes, ma'am." Charlie tipped his hat and grinned. "If I didn't know better I'd say you were Carrie."

Francie bit her lip. She knew he'd meant no harm by it. "I'm not Carrie, and I don't want to be," she said finally, her voice trembling. "Please don't say that again."

Charlie's smile vanished. He swallowed and pulled his hat down so the brim shadowed his eyes. "Sorry, Francie. Guess I didn't think." He moved ahead of her. "If we're going to make it to Connor's Pass and back before dark, we'd best get moving."

The trail to Connor's Pass led through the basin—they followed it in silence. The huge stumps towered over them like giant tombstones. It had been a few years since the loggers had been working in this part of the basin and long grasses and brambles had begun to fill in where once there had been bare forest floor. But Francie found she could easily keep up with Charlie's long strides. Once he turned around, and when he saw her close behind him he raised his eyebrows. He smiled, and Francie thought he was going to say something, but instead he clamped his mouth shut again, turned back, and kept walking.

After they'd been walking for almost an hour, the path forked. One branch headed on through the meadow, weaving its way around the stumps, and the other went up the hill, into forest. Charlie stopped. "You keep up pretty good," he admitted, turning to Francie. He took off his hat and mopped his forehead with his shirtsleeve. "Aren't you hot?"

She sat on a downed log. "Now that you mention it," she said, grinning. "You didn't think I could keep up, did you?"

Charlie shrugged. "I wondered," was all he said. He squinted up the hill. "Connor's Pass is up that way," he said, pointing with his chin. "It ought to be cooler there— we haven't logged in that direction yet and the forest is pretty thick.

"How far until Old Robert's cabin?" Francie looked at the sun, wondering how much daylight was left.

"I don't rightly remember," Charlie answered. "But it must not be too far. We'll get there, but it'll be slower going," he added, examining the steep path ahead of them.

He started up into the woods, and Francie followed him. Here the trees were smaller—young pine and cedar trees and none of the giant sequoias. It was dark and cool, and the red fir and cedars gave off a piney scent that mixed with the damp smell of old leaves and needles. Francie breathed in the earthy perfume and sighed. "Perfect," she said. "I don't blame Old Robert for living up here."

Charlie chuckled. "It's a long way from civilization," he said, grabbing onto a sturdy tree trunk and pulling himself up the steep incline. "No hot baths or home-cooked suppers out here."

Francie just laughed and kept her eyes on the path. Even though there wasn't much underbrush, the path was harder to see. "Not many people come up this far," she said, pointing uphill. "Don't we go that way?"

Charlie scratched his head. "This is the way up to the pass all right, and to Old Robert's cabin, too." He shook his head. "But there aren't many big trees up this way—that's why Connor moved the logging show over to the east end of the basin. I don't see how Carrie's tree could be up here."

Francie pulled out the diary and looked at the entry again. "'I saw Old Robert again today,'" she quoted. "'He took me up over the mountain and showed me my tree. My tree! It is enormous, bigger than any other sequoia in the entire valley. Maybe it's the biggest tree in the entire world!'" She listened to the words as her lips formed them and her voice gave them sound. When she finished the sentence, Carrie's words seemed to hang in the air, and Francie's stomach gave a queer lurch. It was almost as if Carrie herself were there, saying them. Without meaning to, Francie looked around as if she might see Carrie step out from behind a tree.

Charlie was scratching his head. He didn't seem to notice how odd it was to hear Carrie's words spoken here, in her mountains. "I guess 'up over the mountain' could be over Connor's Pass. But there's nothing really to say which mountain she was talking about." He sighed. "It could be anywhere."

Francie refused to become discouraged. "But it makes sense that it's Connor's Pass, since Old Robert lived nearby. He probably knew this mountain better than any other."

"That's true," Charlie admitted. "We can check, anyway." He settled his hat back onto his head and gestured for Francie to go ahead of him.

Under the trees the dim afternoon light was already fading into dusk. Occasionally the trail was crossed by rivulets of running water, turning the steep path into a slippery slide. Francie found herself clutching at the branches of nearby trees to keep her footing. She could hear Charlie grunting.

"Are you sure this trail leads to the pass?" she asked him, stopping to catch her breath. "Nobody must come this way regularly."

"It's one of the more difficult climbs," Charlie said, panting. "It's not dangerous, but it takes a lot of stamina."

"I can see that!" No wonder Carrie was so proud that she'd climbed all the way to the top. "What about the peak? Could we get to the summit today?"

Charlie gave a short laugh. "I don't know about you, but I'm planning to get home in time for supper. The hike to the peak takes two days."

"Carrie did it in one," Francie said, touching the bag. "She says so in her diary."

Charlie gave her an odd look. "I thought you didn't want to compare yourself to Carrie," he said quietly.

"I don't," Francie answered. She felt her cheeks go hot. "I'm not like Carrie."

"So why do you want to climb Connor's Peak?"

Francie closed her eyes. "Because," she said slowly, "because I want to see what she saw." She glanced at Charlie to see if he understood, but he was frowning and looking on up the mountain. How could she explain it when she didn't understand it herself?

"We must be close to Old Robert's cabin," Charlie said. He pushed his hat back off his forehead. "Funny we can't even see a trace of it from here."

About a hundred yards on ahead, the path leveled off. "The pass is that way." Charlie pointed. "And the cabin," he made a quarter turn to the west with his arm straight out in front of him as if he were a living compass, "should be that way." He frowned. "Unless I'm way off in my reckoning."

He moved on, and Francie followed him, wondering how far from the path they would have to go before they found the cabin. Would they lose their way entirely? A

brief vision of her father flashed across her mind. She
shook it away but looked around to find some landmarks
she could remember for later. "This twisted pine," she
whispered, touching the gnarled trunk with her fingertips.
A bit farther on she picked out a large rock about the size
of a footstool. "And there's that fallen log on the left . . .
it'll be to the right on the way back . . ."

If she hadn't been looking so carefully at her surround-
ings, she might not have noticed the mountain dogwood
about twenty-five yards down the mountain from where
she stood. Dogwood! She stopped short. "Charlie, wait!"
She grabbed the diary out of the bag.

"I know I read about it somewhere," she mumbled,
thumbing through the scrawled pages. She headed down
the mountain in the direction of the dogwood tree.

"What's the matter!" Charlie nearly ran into her as he
careened downhill. "Are you hurt?"

Francie looked up. "Dogwood," she said, pointing to
three small trees covered with creamy white blossoms.
"Carrie said there was dogwood growing beside Old
Robert's cabin. She opened the diary and began to read.
"'It's a beautiful place—surrounded with wildflowers.
Dogwood grows all around, and monkeyflower, and a
stunning bunch of phlox where the sun shines most of the
day. You wouldn't expect to find that one in the woods—
not enough light except in that one place.'"

Francie looked around the clearing. Though the sun

had dropped below the tops of the trees, there were the yellow monkeyflowers and pink phlox blooming still. But blackened logs lay all atumble as if some giant hand had scattered them like a child's building blocks. A pile of stones at one end of the clearing was partially covered with vines. "What happened to the cabin?" she whispered.

"Burned down." Charlie pointed to the pile of stones. "Even the chimney fell," he said. "It must have been some blaze!" He looked up as if trying to imagine the flames licking the tops of the trees.

"What do you think happened to Old Robert?"

Charlie's answer was the one that had occurred to Francie as well. "Maybe he was caught inside," he said. "He hasn't been seen around here in years—at least that's what I heard." He walked around the perimeter of what was once a small cabin, kicking charred pieces of wood out of the way and staring down as if he were looking for some sign of the old man.

But Francie quickly stepped outside. "Let's go look for the tree," she said quickly. Somehow it felt wrong to be there, as if she'd been standing on someone's grave.

· Chapter Nine ·

"It might not be around here at all." They had gone over the pass, which was merely a low dip between two peaks. The forest was thick and obscured both the tops of the mountains on either side and the view ahead. Charlie was ready to start back. "If we don't, we'll never get home before dark," he said.

"You go," Francie answered. "I'll just look for fifteen more minutes, and then I'll come."

Charlie watched her in silence. His eyes clouded with a mixture of concern and impatience, and she knew he was thinking of Carrie. She gave him a push. "Go on. I'll probably catch up with you before you get back to the meadow."

She turned away from him to follow a path that was even fainter than the one on the other side of the pass, but before she had taken five steps he was beside her.

"Uncle James would never forgive me if anything happened to you," he said. "We go on for fifteen minutes, and that's all." The firmness of his step as he moved ahead of her said he would not listen to arguments.

"We'll see," she whispered, glad he'd decided to come. But if Charlie heard her he gave no sign.

Francie could see bits of blue sky through the trees, so she knew that out in the meadows and in town it was still afternoon. But here in the forest it was evening—getting darker by the moment. She could hear the contented twitter of birds settling down in the high branches. Squirrels had stopped their scampering and were curling up in their secret holes. With a start she realized that they had moved into a young sequoia grove—the trees were big, but not any bigger than the cedars and pines that shared their space, and they hadn't even developed the shaggy red bark of their mature years. But they were sequoias, and where there were young trees, there must be a mother tree to have cast the seeds.

Francie felt her heartbeat thudding in her throat. The tree *must* be around here. It had to be. Ahead, the path seemed to disappear into a blacker darkness—a protected hollow of the forest where night had already descended or the mouth of an enormous cave.

Charlie's footsteps slowed and then stopped, and she stopped beside him, staring into the darkness. It wasn't a hollow at all or the blackness of night or a cave. They were looking at the largest sequoia tree they'd ever seen—it filled their vision, blocking everything beyond it from their sight, even the late afternoon sunlight.

"Oh, my God," Charlie breathed, taking a step back. "Talk about a giant."

"'The Emperor of Trees,'" Francie whispered, quoting Carrie. She put her hand on her hat to hold it on her head and arched back to see the top, but it was hidden by the smaller trees clustered around it. She moved forward, step-by-step, in silence. Her heart was thudding in her chest and she would hardly have been surprised if the tree had spoken in some huge rumbling voice like an earthquake. This couldn't be real. They must be in some fantasy story.

She reached the tree and, feeling like a tiny elf in a fairy tale, climbed up onto one of the huge buttresses to touch the red fibrous wood. The tree was old beyond imagining. The centuries had cracked and broken the bark until it was shaggy and as full of crevices as the mountainside itself. One enormous fissure was big enough for her to walk into like a cave, and yet compared to the thickness of the tree it was only a small groove. Dark streaks twenty feet above her head showed where a forest fire hundreds of years before had scarred the outer bark. But it was still alive, still growing. She leaned back against the trunk, letting the tree cradle her between its enormous bark ridges. She thought about the tree stump whose rings she'd been counting. "This one must be thousands of years older than that," she murmured, stroking her hand down the ridge next to her arm. "Think of what it has seen."

Charlie was pacing out the circumference of the trunk. "It's more than one hundred feet around!" he shouted. He scrambled up onto the buttress beside Francie, standing with his hands on his hips as he used to do when they were children and played king of the mountain. "This must be the biggest tree in the entire world!"

His eyes were sparkling and he looked the tree up and down as if he were measuring himself against its bulk. "What would it take to bring this one down I wonder."

"What?" The word came out as a small yelp and Francie stood up straight. "What did you say?"

Charlie looked down at her, but he appeared to be seeing something far away. "Bill Weaver is our best faller, and Jim O'Hara is almost as good, but I'd bet they couldn't make the undercut for this monster by themselves. We'd need a whole team of fallers working in shifts." He turned back to the tree. "We'll have to add another length of saw to the biggest one we've got to cut through, and even then . . ." He clapped his hands together and jumped down from the buttress. "But by gum, I'm willing to try!"

Francie stared at him, feeling cold dread move up her arms. Goose bumps rose on her skin. "You're not going to cut this one down," she said quietly. "This is Carrie's tree."

Charlie swung around. "Don't be stupid, Francie. This

is all lumber company land. Of course we'll cut it down."
He grinned at her. "If we do it, we'll be famous!" He
struck a pose with his arm up as if he were showing his
muscles. "The team that brought down the biggest tree on
earth!" He turned back to the tree. "If it doesn't shatter it
could probably supply the wood to build an entire city!"

"No!" Francie stood up on the buttress. "You can't cut
it down. It's probably the oldest thing in the world. It was
growing before . . .," she stuttered, trying to think, "before
Moses, before Abraham." She could feel tears welling up
in her eyes and she shook them away. "How can you even
consider it! This is Carrie's tree!"

Charlie held up his hands. "Calm down. We haven't cut
it down yet."

Francie gathered up her skirts and jumped off, landing
lightly just beside him. "Charlie, if you tell anyone about
this tree Carrie will come back and haunt you. I'll haunt
you. I'll . . ." She searched her mind, trying to think of
something that would stop him.

"Okay, okay." Charlie grinned at her. "I get the point."
He took off his hat, smoothed his hair back, and replaced
the hat on his head. "But the lumber company will find
this tree eventually. It's only a matter of time."

Francie felt the blood rush to her face. "They won't! It's
been here for thousands of years. Carrie knew about it six
years ago and nobody else found out. The only way they'll
know is if you tell them!"

Charlie snorted. "If you're crazy enough to believe that, then the next thing we know you'll be trying to ride the flume." He kicked at one of the cones scattered at the base of the tree and tiny sequoia seeds scattered everywhere. "They haven't been up this way yet because the trees in the rest of the basin are easier to reach. As soon as the company has cut them all, they'll go for the smaller stands and the ones that are harder to get to." He glanced up at the tree. "And they'll come here." He looked down at her, and she thought she could read sadness in his eyes. "They've almost cleared the rest of the basin, Francie," he said softly. "It won't be long. I know what I'm talking about."

Francie sighed. He was right and she knew it. She leaned up against the base of the old tree and crossed her arms. Then she stood up straight. "But the diary said this tree belongs to Carrie. Old Robert left it to her in his will. It doesn't belong to the lumber company. So even if they find it, they can't cut it down."

Charlie was shaking his head again. "Old Robert was a crazy hermit. He probably didn't know what he was talking about. If the lumber company owns the land, then they own the trees, too."

"If!" Francie pointed her finger at him. "If the lumber company owns the land. But maybe they don't. How do you know?"

"They own the whole basin and all the land around it. Everybody knows that. They bought it all just after the government opened up the land for sale."

"That's what everybody says," Francie countered. "But how do you know it's true?"

Charlie sighed. "It's all on record at the land office down in St. Joseph. Go down and take a look if you don't believe me." He squinted up at the fast darkening sky. "If we don't get going it'll be midnight before we get home and Uncle James will have my skin and yours, too!" He turned and headed down the path toward Connorsville.

Francie went past him, stamping her feet with each step. "'Go down and take a look,'" she mumbled. "How can I get to St. Joseph to take a look? Should I just tell my father I'm taking the stage tomorrow? Do you think he'll let me borrow his horse?" She grunted. "Not likely."

Charlie chuckled. "Well, you'll just have to take my word for it, then," he said.

Francie turned to him. "Do I have your word you won't tell anyone about the tree?"

They walked on in silence for a moment. "I reckon," Charlie answered finally. "But as soon as anyone gets wind of it, I'm going to be sure I'm on the team to bring it down. That'll be something to tell my grandchildren about."

Francie looked back. Charlie's head was up and his eyes

were shining in the dim light. Lewis Granger would cut down the tree for the money the lumber might bring. But Charlie would do it for the glory. She bit her lip and looked away. Money and glory. How was she ever going to stop them?

· Chapter Ten ·

By the time they got back to the road leading into Connorsville, the first stars were showing in the sky. "We're never going to make it back in time," said Francie, "unless we run."

Charlie looked at her doubtfully. "Run all the way back to town? You'll never be able to do it. At least, not in that skirt."

Francie knelt on one knee and began untying her heavy walking boots. "You can't tell Papa." She looked up at him. "Promise?"

"Well . . ."

Francie slipped her boots off, stuffed the stockings into them, tied the laces together and slung them around her neck, so they hung down her back. She unpinned her hat and put it into the cloth bag with the diary. "I can't be late. If he gets worried, Papa might not let me come to the woods ever again," she said. She lifted the hems of her ankle-length skirt and petticoat and tucked them into the waistband of her apron so the skirt hung only to her knees. "You've got to promise."

Charlie's eyes widened, watching her. "If Uncle James saw you like that he'd never even let you out of the house again!"

"So do you promise?" The seconds were slipping away.

Finally Charlie grinned. "I promise," he said. Suddenly he grabbed his hat off his head and took off down the road. "And I'll beat you back to town," he called back to her. His boots kicked up dust with each stride.

Francie ran after him, praying that nobody she knew would come down the road at this hour. Her boots flopped against her back. The road was smooth, without many pebbles, and she could feel the cool dirt as she dug in with her toes. She held the cotton bag with the diary close against her side. The trees were turning from green to gray in the dusk, but overhead the sky still glowed blue. She let her breath find an even rhythm and relaxed her shoulders even as she increased her pace. Charlie didn't have much of a lead, and she was closing the space between them with each stride.

When she passed him, he only grunted. She grinned at him. "Hurry up," she said between breaths, and moved smoothly on ahead of him. The coolness of the evening brushed her skin as she ran, and she could smell the scent of wood smoke in the air. She took a deep breath and let it out slowly, remembering how much she used to love racing with Carrie and Charlie. It was one of the few times she could beat them, even though she'd been so much younger.

In ten minutes she was on the edge of town, on the hill above the hotel. Across the street she could see that the lights were on in the kitchen and dining room. "Please let me be on time," she whispered, sitting down in the grass at the edge of the road to put her shoes and stockings back on. She wasn't even breathing that hard.

She put on her hat and was arranging her skirt when Charlie came up beside her. "You're still the fastest runner in town," he said, bending over to catch his breath. "Next Fourth of July you should enter the footraces. I bet you could even beat Buck Murphy."

Francie chuckled, imagining the shocked looks if she showed up at the starting line. "Father would never let me enter," she said.

Charlie slapped his hat back onto his head. "I could have done better without my boots, though. Are we late?"

"I hope not," Francie answered, starting down the hill.

They crossed the street and went around behind the house to the kitchen door. "Mama?" Francie pushed the door open and went in.

Her mother turned from the stove. "There you are," she said. "Supper's almost ready." She looked into the pot and made a face. "In fact, it's more than ready." Then she took a closer look at Charlie. "My goodness! What happened?"

Francie glanced at her cousin in the light from the kerosene lamp on the kitchen table. Lines of dirt streaked his face, and the back of his Sunday shirt was dark with sweat. "Oh," she said quickly, not looking at her mother, "it was warm this afternoon, and we walked a long way." She wiped her own face and wondered if she looked as hot as he did.

"I see," her mother answered.

Francie and Charlie exchanged a glance, and then they both looked at Francie's mother. She was scooping potatoes and carrots into a serving bowl, and Francie wondered exactly how much she did see. "Can you stay for supper, Charlie?" her mother asked.

Charlie had taken his hat off when he came into the kitchen. Now he settled it firmly on his head. "Thank you, Aunt Mary, but I've got to get back to camp. Morning comes early on Monday." He gave her a peck on the cheek. "I'll sure come another time, though."

Francie took off her hat and hung her shoulder bag on a hook by the door, feeling the weight of Carrie's diary as she did so. "Thank you for taking me walking with you, Charlie," Francie said. She wanted to remind Charlie of his promise not to tell about the tree, but she couldn't with her mother right there in the kitchen.

"Anytime, cousin," he said. "It's a pleasure to be with such a refined lady as you." He flashed her a wicked grin and was out the door and down the steps before Francie could say a word.

Francie's mother frowned at his retreating back. "What did he mean by that, I wonder?"

"Pay him no mind," Francie answered, trying to look calm. "He's just teasing." She picked up the bowl of vegetables. "Should I put these on the table?"

"Please," her mother said. "And then run over to the hotel and get your father. I told him he might as well get some work done since this pot roast was taking so long to cook." She gave Francie a significant look. "He's been there all afternoon."

And won't know how late you came home. Francie added the unspoken words to herself. It wasn't any accident that Mama's pot roast took longer than usual to get done. "Thank you, Mama," Francie said, giving her mother a kiss on the cheek. "I'll go get Father."

"Well, it's about time," was all her father said when Francie knocked on his open office door. She watched him go through the familiar routine, closing the ledger and placing it on the shelf with the others, slipping on his suit coat, brushing off imaginary lint, carefully closing and locking the door. "Good night, Herbert," he said, nodding to the desk clerk as they passed through the lobby on their way out.

"Did you and Charlie have a nice afternoon?" Father asked as they walked across the quiet street.

"It was lovely," Francie answered, looking at him out of the corner of her eye. Could she tell him about the tree? Would he know whether it belonged to Carrie? She took a breath. "Father?" Her heart was beating so loud she thought he must be able to hear it.

"Yes?" Her father opened the front door and motioned for her to go in ahead of him.

"Thank you for letting me go with Charlie." She bit her lip. She couldn't do it. Not yet. What if he refused to keep it secret?

"You're welcome," her father said, looking at her. His eyebrows were raised in an unspoken question, but then he turned and went on into the dining room. "Help your mother serve the supper, Frances."

Supper was almost over before Francie decided she would either have to ask the question or burst with the effort of keeping silent. She put down her fork and wiped her lips with her napkin. "Father?"

"Yes?" The look he gave her was distracted.

"Can a person own a tree?"

He frowned. "Of course. We own the trees in front of our house and the ones on the front lawn of the hotel."

Francie tried again. "That's not what I mean. Could a person own one of the sequoias?"

Her father looked at her and then at her mother as if asking for an explanation. Her mother lifted her shoulders slightly and shook her head. "The lumber company owns most of the sequoias," he said. He folded his napkin and placed it by his plate. "Why do you ask?"

Francie swallowed. "Did Carrie own a sequoia tree?"

Her father's face fell into the cold, blank expression it wore whenever Carrie's name was mentioned. "I don't know what you mean, Frances. Of course Carrie never owned a sequoia. How could she?" His voice shook with sudden anger. "What a ridiculous notion!" He pushed his chair back from the table and stood up.

"Wait. Please." Francie turned to her mother. "Old Robert gave Carrie one of the sequoias. Today Charlie and I found it on our walk. It's huge, the biggest tree in the world." Her parents were staring at her, openmouthed. Francie looked from one to the other, knowing she was talking too fast. She wasn't making sense, but she couldn't stop. "It's Carrie's tree. Old Robert left it to her in his will. I know it's hers—Carrie said so. It's in her diary."

The last words fell into profound silence. Francie watched her mother's hands begin to tremble. "Her diary?" her mother whispered. "You found Carrie's diary?"

Francie nodded. "It was . . . in her room." She found she couldn't quite give away Carrie's careful hiding place.

Francie's father grabbed at the tabletop as if to keep himself from falling. Abruptly, he sat back down in his chair. He opened his mouth but then shut it again.

Without saying a word, Francie got up from the table. She walked into the kitchen, got the diary from the shoulder bag, and came back into the dining room. Her steps seemed as loud as gunshots in the quiet room.

"Here it is." She placed the little book in the middle of the table; the dark blue leather looked almost black against the white cloth.

Her parents stared at it. Then her mother turned her head away. "I don't want to read it," she whispered. She was trembling, and she clenched her hands into fists in her lap. "I can't bear it."

Her father cleared his throat. His face was white, but his hand was steady when he picked up the book. "We looked for it after she . . ." He stopped and cleared his throat again. "But we couldn't find it." He looked at Francie. "Have you read it?"

Francie looked at him, and for an instant she thought she saw such pain in his eyes that she wanted to cry out. But then it was gone. She wondered if she'd imagined it. "I've read parts of it," she said. "It's like—"

But her father interrupted, and his voice was sharp. "What about the tree?"

Francie jumped, startled by his anger. "It's the last entry . . ." and her voice faded away, remembering the mention of the White Mountain walking tour. He shouldn't have to read that. "Here." She reached over and took the book from her father's hands.

When she opened it, her mother stood up, pushing her chair back so fast it screeched across the wood floor. "I can't listen," she said. She held her napkin to her face and almost ran from the room. In a moment Francie heard her feet on the stairs. Then in a trembling voice she knew would still sound too much like her sister's, she read Carrie's last entry.

Aug. 13, 1888. I saw Old Robert again today. He took me up over the mountain and showed me my tree. My tree! It is enormous, bigger than any other sequoia in the entire valley. Maybe it's the biggest tree in the entire world! And so old . . . think of the history it has witnessed. I can't fathom it. It is so, so beautiful . . . a Prince among trees. No, a King . . . an Emperor! And I am the steward. No, I am the knight, sworn to protect my Emperor or die in the attempt! Can Old Robert really give me a tree? He says he can . . . he showed me the will and it looks very official. He says I must not tell anyone about this great gift. But how can I keep silent? I am bursting with the joy and the responsibility.

She looked up. Her father sat with his head in his hands; his elbows rested on the table. She wondered if he was crying. "Father?" She reached out, but as she touched his arm he jerked back, away from her.

"And what was your question?" His eyes were red but quite dry. "Could Carrie own that tree?" He shook his head. "Old Robert was a little crazy when it came to the mountains." He smiled, but to Francie it looked more like a grimace. "He used to walk around town shouting about how the lumber company was ruining the mountains. Once he even called down the wrath of God on Thomas Connor." He rubbed his hand across his eyes. "I'm sure he thought he was doing something noble in giving Carrie a tree, and from her words . . ."

His voice broke then. His breath came in a half sob—quickly cut off. With a jerk he stood up and paced over to the sideboard. With shaking hands he began arranging the salt and pepper shakers, the china cups, and little knick-knacks in a line. He picked one up—a delicate china shepherd girl in a light blue dress—and looking fixedly at it rather than at Francie, he continued.

"Your sister was a fanciful child, as her words show. And Old Robert might have truly believed that he was giving her one of the sequoias, but the lumber company owns all that land." Carefully he placed the china girl in line with the others. "Lewis Granger graciously let the poor man live there, but I'm quite sure his cabin was on lumber company land."

Then, still without looking at Francie, he walked out of the room. In a moment Francie heard the front door open and then close again, and she knew he was going back to the hotel.

She sat in the quiet with Carrie's diary in her lap. "I shouldn't have told them," she whispered. "They're still too sad." She blinked away her tears. Her father wouldn't come back until late—he might even work all night. Nothing more would be said about Carrie or about the tree. And especially nothing would be said about the diary. Ever.

She picked up the book and held it to her cheek. This was all that was left of her sister. She opened the book at random and read another entry.

Nov. 30, 1887. It is snowing, and the last of the loggers left a few days ago. There will be no more tourists until spring. Charlie begged his mother to let him stay the winter with us, but the answer was no, as it is every year. So he has to go back to St. Joseph and go to school. Poor Charlie. I would much rather do the lessons Mama makes for us after the hotel closes for the winter than have to leave the mountains and go to school. Winter is one of my favorite times in the mountains— everything is so quiet. As if I am the only person awake in the entire world. After a snowstorm, I am like Eve walking alone through God's creation. Mine are the first footprints ever to mark the new fallen snow.

The next sentence was heavily crossed out—Francie stared at it until her eyes burned, but the words were lost forever. And then Carrie had written the last sentence in an even more scrawled hand than usual.

Papa has FINALLY given me permission to go out. I will take Francie with me. I will be Adam and she can be Eve— we will discover the world together.

Her name, written in Carrie's diary. Francie smoothed it with her finger, as if by touching her name she could somehow touch her sister. She thought she might even be able to remember that day—the snowflakes flying thick, landing on her lashes. The warmth of Carrie's mittened hand holding hers, keeping her from falling as they stomped through the snow, making footprints.

Francie blinked. Her lashes were wet, and it took a moment to realize that they were wet from tears and not snow. She shut the book with a snap. She was just now beginning to discover Carrie's world and she had to do it alone.

She began clearing the table, breaking the silence with the clink of dishes, the clatter of silver as she tossed knives, forks, and spoons into the empty vegetable bowl. She pumped water in the big kettle, and thumped it down onto the stove. She tossed a few more pieces of coal from the coal bucket into the stove and let the iron lid clang down. At least, when her mother crept downstairs in the middle of the night, she'd find the dishes already washed, dried, and put away.

After she went up to her room, she opened the secret hiding place in the wardrobe and placed the diary inside. "I need you, Carrie," she whispered, smoothing the soft leather cover. She lowered the false bottom and closed the wardrobe doors. "I don't think I can do this by myself, and there's nobody here to help me."

It wasn't until she was in bed and drifting toward sleep that her father's words came back to her. "I'm quite sure his cabin was on lumber company land." He hadn't said, "Robert's cabin *was* on lumber company land." Somehow, the way he'd added, "I'm quite sure" suddenly sounded to Francie almost as if he wasn't really sure at all. But before she could examine that thought more carefully, she was asleep.

· Chapter Eleven ·

"Three thousand, two hundred and fifty-one. Three thousand, two hundred and fifty-two," Francie said and put her finger on the tiny circle of wood in the exact center of the old stump. "Three thousand, two hundred and fifty-two." She said it again out loud even though there was nobody else in the basin to hear her—only the squirrel who kept scurrying up the trunk to check on her and then scrambling down whenever she made a face at him. Did trees feel? Could they think? Did this one have any idea what was happening when Bill Weaver or whoever was the faller made that first chop with his ax into its bark?

She looked to the north and with her eyes she followed the path that wound through the basin, the same path that yesterday had led her to Carrie's tree. How old was that one? Would they cut it down, too, with as little care as they had for this one? She knew they would, if they found out about it. She closed her eyes and said a little prayer that Charlie would keep this secret. He was good at keeping secrets—hadn't Carrie said so in her diary?

The cotton shoulder bag was lying beside her in a puddle of soft gray fabric that outlined the shape of the diary inside it. She had been going to keep it in the hiding place, never take it out again. But somehow, she couldn't. "Not yet," she whispered. She slid it out of the bag, and then searched around until she found the pencil she'd decided at the last moment to bring. She opened the book to Carrie's last entry, and then turned one page.

June 16, 1894.

Her hand was shaking; she put the pencil down and wiggled her fingers. Then she began again.

Dear Carrie
Today I finished counting the rings on the old sequoia stump, the first one they cut in Connor's Basin. It was three thousand two hundred and fifty-two years old. I shall write Mr. Court a letter telling him. I haven't seen any of his articles because Father takes the newspaper to work with him. I think he does it on purpose, so I can't read them. He's letting me count the rings on the stump, but he won't let me say anything against the logging.

• • •

She stopped, read the words she'd just written, and then smoothed the page with the side of her hand. If she were alive, Carrie would be furious to find her sister writing in her diary. But now . . . Francie bent her head and finished her first entry.

Someday soon I will climb Connor's Peak. Like you, Carrie.

She lifted her head again, an idea bubbling inside her. Suddenly she couldn't write fast enough.

In fact, I will go to all the places you went. I'll write about what I see. It won't be what you saw, because of the logging. But I'll try to imagine it the way you saw it.
That's all for now.
Love,
Francie

P.S. Please don't be mad at me for writing in your diary.

Francie closed the book, feeling a little silly. It wasn't as if Carrie could actually read when Francie wrote, could know what she was thinking. She sighed. "I wish she could read it and answer and tell me what to do." The squirrel had been sitting on the top rung of the ladder, watching her. At the sound of her voice he dropped his acorn and disappeared over the side of the stump. She leaned over the edge to watch him scamper down. "Why don't you tell me what to do," she called after him.

She sat with her legs hanging over the edge of the stump and looked at the diary. She'd wanted to climb to the top of Connor's Peak to read Carrie's words, but according to the diary, it was an all-day climb. Carrie hadn't minded missing supper, but Francie didn't dare risk it. This would have to do. She opened the book again.

June 16, 1887. Francie stared at the date. Carrie had written it exactly seven years earlier on this very day, when she'd decided to fill up Carrie's empty pages. The thought came with a shiver of goose bumps up her arms. She read on:

> *I saw Old Robert today—just a glimpse of his battered hat and torn coat through the trees as I was walking down Connor's Creek. That means he survived another winter. I'm glad. Someday I will find out where he goes. He told me once that he hibernates. He couldn't have been serious . . . but with Old Robert you never know. He's a strange creature— indeed, almost like a bear at times.*

Francie closed the diary, keeping her finger between the pages to mark the place. It was a little like reading a novel. If she kept on, would she find the truth about the tree and Old Robert?

• • •

June 21, 1887. Today I visited Old Robert at his cabin. It was truly an honor—he saw me in the basin and invited me to tea! His voice was cracked and gravely as if he hadn't used it much, but he has such a nice smile. I said yes, and then, without a word, he turned and marched off. I followed him up Connor's Creek—his cabin is about an hour's walk from the basin, near the place where the creek forks. It's a beautiful place—surrounded with wildflowers. Dogwood grows all around and monkeyflower and a stunning bunch of phlox in one place where the sun shines most of the day. You wouldn't expect to find that one in the woods—not enough light except in that one place. Old Robert boiled the water in an old kettle over a tiny iron stove and served the tea in two delicate china cups. Why do you suppose he has china cups in a rugged mountain cabin? When I asked him, he acted as if I had not spoken at all. But he did ask me to visit again. I think I will. He has two books on a corner shelf in his cabin—the Bible and Shakespeare's sonnets. He can recite both from memory. It was quite amazing, this old bear of a man quoting Shakespeare's love poetry.

July 1, 1887. Today I took Old Robert a packet of black tea—his favorite kind, as he told me. He was in a foul mood—shaking his fists and shouting out about robbery and the sheriff and "hanging the devil." He was so angry I was almost afraid of him. He growled and grumbled and paced up and down from one side of the small cabin to the other. His speech is hampered by his lack of teeth, and I couldn't understand all he said, but it seemed he was upset by the idea that the lumber company was going to start logging the sequoia trees. It's curious how surprised he was . . . as if he didn't know it would happen eventually. Wasn't that the whole reason Connor had purchased the land? I tried to point it out to him, but he turned on me and called me a murderer! "Sequoias aren't killed by disease and they don't burn," he yelled at me. "Don't you know that if men didn't cut them down they'd live forever?" I said I'd stop the logging if I could. At least he quieted then, and stroked my head with his hand. As if I were the one who needed calming. What a strange old man. He said something odd then, odder even than his usual mumblings. "I'm the one can stop it, Missy," he said. "And I will, too. You just wait and see." I wish it were true. There's something terrible about logging the sequoias. Robert is right about them living forever—I read about that in a book. There's something in the bark that protects them against fire and disease, and insects don't bother them the way they do other trees. They're almost immortal—like the angels. Does that mean when someone cuts one down, it's like killing an angel?

July 3, 1887. Robert came to the hotel today! What a change! His hair was washed and brushed, and he was wearing a suit! It was old and out of fashion, but it was clean—he

*must have put it away somewhere in his cabin waiting for a
special occasion. He asked Papa if he could speak to me for a
moment, and Papa agreed, though the look he gave me was
very suspicious. Old Robert told me he was going to St. Joseph
to see to that problem we talked about. He must have meant
the logging, but he wouldn't say it outright, and he wouldn't
let me say it, either. It was just like a dime novel—very exciting and mysterious! Father asked me many questions about
him at supper, but I didn't give anything away.*

*July 4, 1887. The entire town picnicked in Connor's Basin
today to celebrate Independence Day. Thomas Connor made
a speech, long and boring. He is the most pompous man I've
ever seen. And Lewis Granger always stands beside him like
some kind of bodyguard. "A man can smile and smile and be
a villain."* Doesn't that come from Hamlet? *Shakespeare
would have recognized Granger in a moment. That man
gives me the shivers.*

"Me, too," Francie said, nodding. It felt good to find she
and Carrie agreed about something. She skipped Carrie's
description of the people at the picnic and turned the pages,
looking for another entry about Old Robert. But her eye
was caught by the mention of her own name again.

*September 14, 1887. I WISH Papa would stop worrying so
much. He knows I can take care of myself in the mountains.*

And Francie can do the same. She's as surefooted as a little mountain goat and has the balance of one as well. Papa keeps saying, "It's not proper for a young woman." If he'd wanted us to be proper, why didn't he take us all back East and open a hotel in Philadelphia! Please don't let him think about that—I would die in Philadelphia!

The words on the page blurred as Francie's eyes filled with tears. Carrie had thought she was as surefooted as a mountain goat! "I wish you'd have said that to me, Carrie," Francie said aloud. "Why did you always have to tease?"

"Because that was her way. She teased everyone."

Francie jerked violently and bit off a scream as she saw Charlie standing just below her, leaning up against the ladder. "Charlie! You scared me almost to death." Then she realized the significance of his presence. "It's after six o'clock?" She closed the diary, grabbed the shoulder bag, and scrambled down the ladder almost as fast as the squirrel. "I'm going to be late again."

"Aunt Mary sent me to find you. She said you'd be out here." He tapped the diary. "Find anything else interesting in there?"

"Lots. Listen to this." She opened the book.

May 15, 1887. Charlie comes tomorrow. I can hardly wait a moment longer. There is so much to show him. First the fox pups. And then the cave. He'll love it—we can camp there after it gets warmer. Elizabeth Jordan thinks I'm silly to be best friends with a boy, and one who is two years younger. But I think Elizabeth Jordan is a fool. Charlie's the best, best cousin and the best, best friend in the world.

"I was twelve," Charlie said after a moment. His eyes looked sad. He reached over Francie's shoulder and began picking pieces of bark off the old stump with his fingernail. "I lived for summers back then."

"And now Elizabeth Jordan would do just about anything for a smile from you," Francie said, sorry she'd read him the entry.

Charlie gave Francie the smile Elizabeth Jordan would die for. "Carrie was right. Elizabeth Jordan is a fool." He dusted off his hands. "Anything about Old Robert?"

"I was just looking." She read him the entries she'd found so far, and then thumbed through the remaining pages. "Here's one."

December 15, 1887. The blizzard is over and I went to the woods this afternoon. I was tempted to go all the way to Old Robert's cabin. (Does he stay in that little cabin all winter? He couldn't. He wouldn't have enough food, would he?) But in the end, there wasn't time. I'll have to go visit the old man another day.

• • •

"That's the only thing I can find—just little comments about unimportant things." She shut the book and gave it a little shake. "Nothing more about why he was dressed up so fine or what happened in St. Joseph." She looked up at Charlie. "Maybe that's when he had the will made."

Charlie gave her an almost pitying look. "He was a crazy old man."

"Even crazy old men make wills," she retorted.

Charlie squinted up at the sky. "You ready to head back home? I'm staying for supper, in case you didn't know, and I'm getting hungry."

Francie grinned at him. "Shall we run back?"

He laughed and, tipping his hat, offered her his arm. "Not a chance. Will you *walk* with me back to town?"

"With pleasure, sir," Francie answered, curtsying.

· Chapter Twelve ·

"I wanted to be absolutely certain I gave you correct information last night," said Francie's father, "so I asked Lewis about individuals owning sequoia trees." He took a sip of his after-dinner coffee and looked at Francie. "I assume Charlie is familiar with the subject as well?"

Francie stared at her father. In honor of Charlie's visit she'd also been allowed to have coffee, well laced with thick cream. Now she clattered the cup back onto its saucer with trembling fingers. "You didn't tell Mr. Granger about Carrie's tree, did you?" She felt as if the floor had suddenly given way beneath her chair.

Her father frowned. "Of course. I asked about the trees and the land on the north side of the basin. I told him my daughter had discovered an especially big tree up by Connor's Pass where the old hermit used to live and had the strange idea that Old Robert owned the land rather than the lumber company. I asked if that was even possible."

Charlie cleared his throat. "What did he say, Uncle James?" He glanced at Francie and then away again.

Francie's father stroked his mustache with his finger. "He took me into the lumber company office and asked me to show him on the map where the tree was." He shrugged. "I didn't know exactly, but from the entry in the diary—"

"You read Carrie's diary?" Charlie's eyebrows went up.

"Frances read me the one entry," Francie's father said stiffly. "I assume the tree must be up by Connor's Pass, since that's all unexplored land. But," and he tapped his finger on the white tablecloth, "my answer to you yesterday was correct. The lumber company owns all that land. Old Robert may have wished to deed the tree to Carrie, but it wasn't his to give away."

"But what about the will?" Francie gripped the tabletop so hard her fingers turned white. "Carrie saw the will!"

Francie's father reached out and touched Francie's hand. "He may not have understood the law, Frances," he said. "Everyone said he wasn't always right in his head. He may have thought since he lived on the land, he owned it. But Mr. Granger assured me that wasn't the case here."

Francie held her breath, trying not to cry. She looked at her father's hand covering her own. A question was buzzing in her brain, one she didn't want to know the answer to, but she had to ask it anyway. "Papa," she began in a small voice, "did Mr. Granger seem interested in the tree?"

"The discovery of a tree that big is always of interest to the lumber company, Frances," her father said. "Because of the depression, Connor isn't as solid as he'd like to be. The more wood he cuts, the more he'll sell, and the stronger the company will become. Any new stands are of help." He patted her hand and then began folding up his napkin.

Francie stood up. "He can't cut that tree, Father." She was surprised to find her voice almost steady. "That's Carrie's tree. She promised to protect it."

Her father sighed. "Frances, I know you love the trees, and I know Carrie did. But we can't let our personal preference stand in the way of human progress. The decision to cut the tree will be made by Granger."

"James, is there no possibility they'll leave it alone?" Francie's mother put her hand to her mouth, and Francie knew it was to hide the quivering of her lips. "If Carrie loved it . . ."

"Now don't you start, Mary." Francie's father stood up. "It's enough to drive a man mad, all these softhearted women. What do you think, Charlie?"

Charlie looked at him and swallowed nervously. "I guess I just don't know, sir. It would be a great challenge to bring it down in one piece, and I think we've got the man-power to do it." Then his eyes met Francie's. "But it would be a shame, too, in a way. It's so old."

"Think of how many years it's been growing, Papa." Francie rushed around the table and grabbed his arm. "That stump had more than three thousand rings. This one is probably even older than that. Can't you stop them? Can't you do this for Carrie? So we have something to remember her by?"

Francie's father closed his eyes and his face looked sud-denly gray and old. "I don't want to remember," he mumbled. He tried to pull away, but Francie was holding onto his arm. He looked down, but instead of brushing her hand away as she'd expected, he covered it with his own. They stood there in silence for a moment. Then, gently, he lifted her hand, touched it to his cheek, and then let go and walked out of the room. Francie waited, looking at her mother's stricken face and Charlie's sad eyes. In a moment the front door opened and then closed again.

"He's going back to the hotel," Francie's mother said. She sighed and began clearing away the dishes. She looked up at Francie. "Don't be angry with him. You don't understand how he feels."

Francie shook her head. "You're right. I don't. I miss Carrie, too, but how can he just—"

Charlie stood up, interrupting her. "I've got to go, Francie. Walk me to the door?"

Francie looked at him and then at her mother, standing with bowed head and a pot in her hand. She bit her lip. "Of course," she said.

When they were out in the hall, he turned to her. "Let it be, Francie. You can't change them. Only time will do that."

"It's been six years!" Francie whispered, but it felt as if she were shouting. "How much longer will it take?" Tears that had been burning in her eyes since her father's announcement spilled over. "And now he won't even fight to save Carrie's tree."

"We don't know if it's Carrie's tree," Charlie murmured. He touched her shoulder. "And maybe Granger won't bother with it. There's plenty of logging still left to do on the east side."

"It doesn't matter whether Carrie owns it." Francie almost shouted, and Charlie put his finger on her lips. "It doesn't matter," she began again more softly. "Why can't he fight anyway? For me! Why can't he fight for what I want?"

She wiped her wet cheeks with the back of her hands. "And you think Granger won't bother with that tree? Ha! The chances of that are about the same as me riding the flume. You said it yourself when we found it. You just wait, Charlie Spencer. Granger will want that tree. He'll be angling to cut it down as soon as possible. And then there won't be anything of Carrie left in the entire world." She put her hands over her face and sobbed.

"Francie?" Charlie's voice was hesitant. She felt his hand on her shoulder tighten, and then he sighed. He put his arms around her, holding her as if she were made out of glass and might break at the least movement. "Just cry it out, cuz," he said, stroking her hair. "It's okay."

· Chapter Thirteen ·

By the next afternoon, Connorsville was buzzing with the news. A giant sequoia—the biggest on earth—had been found just over the top of Connor's Pass. Francie was changing the sheets in room 30 when Charlie stuck his head around the doorjamb.

"Don't say a word about it," she said quickly, taking in his raised eyebrows and sparkling eyes. She bent to tuck the ends of the bottom sheet neatly around the end of the feather bed. "I've heard more than I want to already. I think every single guest in the hotel ordered a box lunch to take up to Connor's Pass."

Charlie came into the room, dusted off his pants, and sat down on the chair. "The photographer's shop is doing a whopping business. John's set up his camera by the tree and is charging seventy-five cents a photo." He shook his head. "He's getting it, too. They all want a picture of themselves beside the oldest living thing in the world."

"Why aren't you working?" Francie spread the blanket over the sheets and plumped up the pillows.

"Got the day off."

Francie gave him a sharp look, and he nodded, answering her unspoken question. "We're moving to the north end of the basin tomorrow. Gonna start logging around the big one, Granger says. Clear everything out around it, and then see if we can bring it down."

Francie plopped down on the newly made bed. "You can't. It'll shatter. It's too big."

Charlie stroked his chin and shrugged. "Some think that," he agreed. "But Granger says it's worth the risk. If we can bring it down whole, think of how much lumber we'll have." He closed his eyes. "Not quite a city's worth—but close. Think of it, Francie, an entire city built from one tree. It'll put California on the map for certain." He stood up. "Nobody will be able to argue that we don't grow things bigger and better than anywhere else in the whole United States of America."

Francie watched him, feeling numb. "Is that what you think?"

He looked at her. "Truth?"

She nodded.

He scratched his head. "Truth is . . ." He paused, took a breath, and began again. "Truth is, I don't know what to think. Think of a whole city built from one tree." He thumped his chest. "One I could help bring down. It's a chance in a lifetime. And it's only one tree. There are hundreds more."

Francie sprang to her feet. "But such a tree!" she cried. "It isn't *only* one tree. There is *only* one tree as big or as old as that one. How can you even think to cut it down?"

"But trees grow back, Francie."

Francie gave a short laugh. "Yes, they grow back. In three thousand years. I counted the rings on that stump, remember? And besides," she said sadly, "Granger isn't cutting *only* this one tree. He's cutting all the trees." She turned, but not before Charlie saw her tears.

"Okay," he said. "It's too bad. But it's not your fault. It's not you cutting the tree."

"But it is my fault." She looked over at him. "If I hadn't found that note or the diary, if I hadn't been so sure we had to find this secret of Carrie's," she kicked the bedstead hard enough to make her foot ache, "if I hadn't asked my father about it. Then nobody would even know about the tree. It would be safe."

Charlie shook his head. "You're wrong. Maybe it would be safe for this year, but what about next year or the year after? Someday, Granger would have found that tree. Depend upon it."

Francie didn't listen to him. "I had a thousand chances to stop. But I didn't. I had to keep on poking around until I found it. And then I had to ask my father." She picked up a pillow, punched it hard, and then put it back on the bed.

"You already did that," Charlie said.

She turned on him, almost snarling. "Already did what?"

Charlie grinned. "You already plumped up that pillow." He pointed to it.

"Oh." Francie pulled on a corner of the pillow to straighten it. "Don't think you can make me laugh and forget about this because you can't." She picked up the empty wicker basket she'd carried the clean sheets in. "I'm finished here. Are you coming?" And without looking to see if he was following her, she left the room.

The lobby was full of guests drinking tea and eating the vanilla shortbread her mother baked every Tuesday morning. The words "biggest tree in the world" and "oldest thing on earth" drifted in the air, and Francie walked through the crowd as fast as she could. She didn't want to hear anything more about Carrie's tree.

"You'd think with all those people so excited about that tree," she grumbled, hanging the basket on its hook in the linen room, "that someone might think about whether or not it ought to be cut down!"

Charlie jumped out of her way as she swept out of the linen room and into the kitchen. "Maybe you should talk to them, try to get them to stop the lumber company."

She turned around and stared at him. "Now that's the most sensible thing I've heard you say in a long time."

"Francie . . ." Her mother, who was stirring something in an enormous kettle at the back of the stove, frowned at her. "I'm sure your father wouldn't appreciate you badgering the guests."

"I won't badger them. I'll just talk to them." She grabbed up an extra plate of vanilla shortbread, took a deep breath, and marched into the lobby.

"Good afternoon, Francie." Old Mrs. Evans was perched on a straight-backed chair by the refreshment table.

"Good afternoon, Mrs. Evans." Francie picked up the half full plate of shortbread and placed her own full plate in its place. "Did you go out to see the big tree?"

Mrs. Evans gave a raspy chuckle and reached for a fresh piece of shortbread. "Not on these old legs," she said, patting her lap. "I'm satisfied to walk from the lobby to my room each evening." Mrs. Evans and her husband had been coming to the hotel each summer as long as Francie could remember. "I used to be able to ramble over the mountains," she said, "but now I'm content to just breathe in the good mountain air." She took a deep breath as if to prove her words true.

"Don't you think it's a shame the lumber company is planning to cut down that tree?" Francie said. "It's so old and all." She looked at Mrs. Evans's wrinkled face and suddenly realized she might take offense. "I mean . . ." she began again, stuttering.

Mrs. Evans looked up at her; her faded blue eyes were amused and sad at the same time. "The old must give way to the new," she said. "You young ones will build us an entirely new world." She nodded and looked away. "It's the same with trees as it is with men." She chewed a bite of shortbread. "You tell your ma she's the best shortbread baker in the state of California." Her eyes twinkled and she took another bite.

"Yes, ma'am," Francie answered. She sighed and turned away. If everyone agreed with Mrs. Evans, her plan was doomed to failure from the start.

Her father was standing in the middle of the room, his thumbs tucked into the pockets of his waistcoat. He was surrounded by a group of guests, and Mr. Mansfield was gesturing with the stem of his pipe. "You mark my words," he was proclaiming, "Connor isn't going to let this depression beat him. He'll make thousands on that tree. It's the best thing that's happened to this area in a long time." Mr. Mansfield always sounded as if he were speech making. Father said he was thinking of running for Congress.

"You don't have to convince me," Father answered him.

Francie didn't stay to hear more. It was clear she wouldn't make any headway with that group. She scanned the room. Gloria Mansfield, wife of the would-be congressman, was ensconced on the medallion-back sofa Father had had shipped from New York two years ago. Its pale rose material nicely complemented Mrs. Mansfield's burgundy shirtwaist, and Francie suspected she'd chosen the seat for that very reason. Three young and admiring women were sitting on chairs around her listening to her words as if she were a queen.

What did Mrs. Mansfield think, Francie wondered. She might be a powerful ally. She gripped the plate with both hands and walked over to the group. "More shortbread?" she asked, offering each woman in turn.

"Thank you, Francie." Mrs. Mansfield took a small piece. "Could we have some more tea as well?"

"Yes, ma'am." Francie left the shortbread on the small table beside the sofa, picked up the tray full of empty teacups, and returned to the kitchen.

"Mrs. Mansfield's group wants more tea," she told her mother, who was pouring boiling water over the tea leaves in one of their large porcelain teapots. "Where's Charlie?"

"Went out the back door," her mother answered. "He said something about work waiting."

"Pooh," Francie said. She filled the sink with dirty dishes and placed clean cups and their saucers on the tray. "He just doesn't want to make small talk in the lobby." She leaned against the counter while she waited for the tea to steep.

"You're not talking about that tree, are you?" her mother asked. She bit her lip and looked at Francie. "Your father will be so distressed if you upset the guests."

"Mama, nobody talks of anything *but* the tree," Francie

said. "How big it is, if they'll be able to cut it down, how many houses it will build . . ." She sighed. "It's hopeless. I wish I'd never found it."

The sad expression on Francie's mother's face told her that her mother wished it, as well. "This is ready, now," was all she said as she placed the teapot in the exact middle of the tray among the teacups.

Francie gave her mother a kiss on the cheek. "Thank you, Mama," she whispered. She picked up the tray and went out to the lobby.

"Here you are," she said to Mrs. Mansfield, sliding the tray onto the low table in the middle of the group of women. "Would you like me to pour you a cup?"

"Yes, please, Francie." Mrs. Mansfield picked up a cup and held it out. "I understand you're the one who found that huge tree," she said, looking up. Was it Francie's imagination that she didn't look entirely happy about it?

"Yes, ma'am," Francie said. "Though my sister found it first, years ago," she added.

"Your sister?" One of the young women sitting by Mrs. Mansfield raised her eyebrows. "I didn't know you had a sister. Where is she?"

Francie couldn't remember the woman's name, Mrs. Lockridge, or something like that. "My sister was killed in a landslide six years ago," she answered, feeling as if her face had turned to wood. Six years and still she never knew what to say when people asked her that. She turned away.

The three other women murmured soft words of comfort too quietly for Francie to really hear what they'd said. "Mary," Mrs. Mansfield's voice was gently scolding, "I told you that when you arrived. Don't you remember?"

Out of the corner of her eye she saw Mary's face flush slightly. "Oh, I beg your pardon. Please don't be offended. I'm so silly about things like that." She was speaking too fast and Francie felt sorry for her. She turned back to fill her cup with tea.

"But aren't you excited about that enormous tree?" The woman was rattling on. "It even looks ancient, don't you think? People are saying it's the oldest thing on earth. Think of that." She took a sip of tea. "Gerald," she looked at Mrs. Mansfield, "that's my husband, Gerald." She turned back to Francie and the other women. "Gerald has agreed to buy some of the lumber. We're planning to build a house in St. Joseph next year. I think it would be so romantic if the whole house were built from that one tree. Imagine. We'd be surrounded by three-thousand-year-old wood." She raised her head. "Much older than any English castle." She took another sip of her tea.

Mrs. Mansfield shook her head. "Well, I think it's a shame," she said. She glanced at her husband, still speech making in the center of the room. "Glen doesn't agree with me, of course. He thinks cutting the tree will liven up the economy in this area." She looked up at Francie. "But I'm almost sorry you discovered it."

Francie's heart seemed to take a giant leap; she thought she might lean down and kiss Mrs. Mansfield, and almost laughed out loud as she imagined the woman's surprised face if she actually did it. "I am, too," Francie said, trying to speak calmly. "I wish I could do something to stop them from cutting it down." She gripped the teapot hard with both her trembling hands.

Mrs. Mansfield looked at the women around her. "Someone should write to Frank Court, the editor of the *St. Joseph Herald.* He's violently opposed to logging in this area, especially the sequoias. I'm sure that if he knew about it, he'd certainly try to do something." She put her empty teacup down on the tray beside the pot. "I can't do it myself, because of my husband's position, of course." She shook her head. "He'd be absolutely furious if I did something like that."

The women all nodded wisely, even Mary, now looking even more embarrassed about her dream of a house built of sequoia wood than she did about her tactless words to Francie. "Of course you can't do that," she said. "But someone should."

They seemed to have forgotten Francie, who placed the teapot carefully on the tray and moved away as unobtrusively as she could. "Mr. Court," she mumbled. "Of course! And I have to write him, anyway." She rubbed her hands down the sides of her apron. It was going to work! She was going to save the tree.

· Chapter Fourteen ·

The letter had been easy to write. More difficult was the problem of getting it to St. Joseph. The stage, which took the mail and passengers to St. Joseph, had already left and wouldn't be back again until Friday. Francie considered the creamy white envelope lying flat on her vanity. When was her father next going to St. Joseph? Perhaps he would take it with him.

"I *was* going tomorrow morning," he told her when she found him in his office at the hotel. "But I lent the mare to Hopkinson yesterday, and she went lame. It'll be two weeks before she's sound enough to ride." He sounded disgusted. "I should know better than to lend my horse away. Even to Hopkinson." He grunted, and then looked up at Francie. "Why do you ask?"

Francie held up the letter. "I want to get this to Mr. Court." She saw her father's eyebrows begin to draw together in a frown, but she went on. She'd already decided what to say—she might as well get it over with. "I finished counting the rings of that tree and I feel it's important he get the information as soon as possible." It wasn't a lie, she told herself. She did write about the 3,252 rings. But she also told him what was happening with Carrie's tree.

Francie met her father's eyes with what she hoped looked like confidence, but inwardly she was shaking. Would he refuse to let her send the letter?

Her father drummed his fingers on the desktop, and then sighed. "I suppose I did give you permission to do this. So we might as well finish the job." He held out his hand for the letter. "I'm sure I can find someone who's going to St. Joseph in the next few days."

Francie clutched the letter. "It's important that the letter get there tomorrow."

Her father raised one eyebrow. "Why the hurry? Those articles of his come out every week like clockwork. What's the difference between one week and another?"

Francie sighed. She'd anticipated this question, as well. "It took me longer than he'd expected to count the rings," she explained. "When he was here he told me he needed the information by the beginning of June, and it's the middle of June already." She put her hand on the doorknob. "I'll see if I can find someone else who's going tomorrow."

"Frances." The stern tone in her father's voice stopped her. "I will find someone to take the letter tomorrow," he said. "And if I can't I will let you know." He put his hand out for the letter again. "I am just as honest as you are, Daughter, and just as eager to keep my promises."

He didn't smile, but as Francie put the letter into his hand she felt that his face had softened, that he might smile any moment. "Yes, Papa," she said, kissing the top of his head. "I trust you."

He grunted again. "But this does not mean that I've changed my mind about the logging."

"No, Papa," Francie answered again. She bobbed a little curtsy, which made her father almost snort. He waved his hand, dismissing her, and she practically skipped out of the hotel. Her letter would get to Mr. Court tomorrow. As soon as he heard what was happening he would come as fast as he could. He'd get here on Wednesday. She closed her eyes. "Please let that be soon enough," she prayed in a whisper.

But Wednesday came, and Mr. Court didn't. It had taken Francie all day to make up the beds on the street side of the hotel because she spent most of the time watching out the window. But the only buggies she saw belonged to people who lived in Connorsville or guests at the hotel.

"What's taking you so long?" her mother said when she finally came to find Francie. "Josie finished ages ago and you still have two rooms to do!"

Francie had been staring at the street, trying to will Mr. Court's buggy into view; she jumped when she heard her mother's voice and dropped the pile of sheets she'd been holding. "I'm sorry, Mama," she answered. "I'm almost finished." She picked up the sheets, piled them into her basket, and sank down into a chair. Then she popped up again and glanced out the window when she heard the *clop-clop* of horses' hooves approaching the hotel. "It's only old Mrs. Winters," she mumbled, turning back to her mother.

Her mother came into the room, looked out the window herself, and then turned back to Francie. "Are you expecting someone? Is that why you told Josie you'd do all the rooms on this side of the hotel today? Who did you think would be coming?"

Francie's mind went blank. "Nobody," she answered too quickly. "Who would be coming?" She stared at her mother as if daring her to ask more questions.

Her mother looked at her curiously, but then she shrugged. "The new guests will want to get into their rooms soon, so let Herbert know as soon as you're finished." Her mother's trust made Francie almost break down and confide everything. But she couldn't. If her father found out what she'd done, he'd tell Mr. Granger. And somehow she knew that if Lewis Granger thought someone was trying to stop him cutting that tree, he'd bring it down even sooner. She couldn't take the chance.

Francie's mother was almost out the door when she turned around. "Charlie is coming for supper this evening. He was in town earlier, and your father invited him."

"Why wasn't he working?" Francie wondered aloud.

Her mother shook her head. "You can ask him yourself when he comes," she said. "Now I have some chores to do in the kitchen."

Francie frowned. Maybe they'd stopped work at the big tree. Maybe Mr. Court had come and she'd missed seeing him. Her heart lifted a bit and she finished making the bed in a rush.

Even though she was hurrying now, it took her almost until suppertime to finish her chores. In fact, her mother was putting supper on the table when she arrived. Charlie was already sitting at his place at the table, talking with her father.

"We're clearing the area in record speed," Charlie was saying as Francie brought in a bowl full of boiled potatoes. "All the smaller trees around the big one have to come down—we're making a 'featherbed' of all the branches to cushion the big one's fall. It's on a downhill slope, but Granger is determined to bring it down in one piece." He couldn't hide the excitement in his voice, but at least the look he gave Francie as she sat down was tinged with guilt.

"How much longer?" she asked, feeling as if she were sitting at the bedside of a dying patient.

Charlie shook his head. "Couple of days at least."

Francie's mother came into the room carrying a platter of sliced roast beef. "I carved it in the kitchen," she said, looking at Francie's father. "I hope you don't mind—it makes such a mess on the tablecloth when you carve it at the table." She placed the platter in front of him and sat down in her place.

"Have they started the undercut?" Francie's father asked as he began to spoon meat and potatoes on each plate. "I'd think it would take quite a while, seeing how massive the tree is."

"Thank you," Charlie said, taking the plate Francie's father handed to him. "We'll start tomorrow afternoon or Friday. Granger was shooting for tomorrow morning, but the team hasn't even been chosen yet."

The food suddenly turned dry as dust in Francie's mouth. Tomorrow! Unless Mr. Court showed up early in the morning, Carrie's tree would be cut and nothing Francie could do would stop them.

"Why were you in town today, then?" she asked Charlie. "Surely you'll be trying to get on the team." She knew her tone was bitter, but she couldn't help it any more than Charlie could help his own excitement.

Charlie glanced quickly at her father and then at her. "I had some errands in town," he said. "Cook needed some . . . supplies and stuff." His answer was vague to the point of being odd. It was unusual for the loggers to come to town at all during the week, let alone in the middle of the day, but the furious look he gave Francie stopped her from asking any more questions.

She didn't want to ask any more questions. She didn't want to know anything more about what was happening to Carrie's tree. It was going to be cut down—the oldest thing on earth. She kept her eyes on her plate, hoping that the others could not see her tears, and put one bite after another into her mouth. She chewed and swallowed, but everything tasted like sawdust.

As soon as everyone was finished eating she stood up. "May I be excused?" she said. Her mother looked at her with pleading in her brown eyes, as if she were asking for something that Francie couldn't give, and finally nodded.

"I have to be going, too." Charlie quickly pushed his chair back and stood up. "Walk me to the door, Francie?"

Francie had turned to go upstairs, but his words stopped her. She looked over at him, feeling the hope rise in her chest. "Of course," she said. Maybe he did have some news after all.

"That was a delicious meal, as usual, Aunt Mary." Charlie gave Francie's mother a kiss on the cheek and shook hands with Francie's father. He nodded to Francie and she led the way out of the dining room.

Charlie walked behind her in silence, but when they were at the front door Francie couldn't wait any longer. "Did Mr. Court come to the logging camp today?"

Charlie raised his eyebrows. "Not that I know of. Was he supposed to?"

Francie's heart suddenly felt as if it were made of lead. "I wrote him a letter," she began in a small voice. "I was hoping he'd make it here in time to stop them cutting Carrie's tree. I thought that was why you came to town."

Charlie shook his head. He opened the door, motioned her to go ahead of him, and they both went out on the front porch. "I wanted to let you know what was happening—how close we were." He shoved his hands into his pockets. "If there's anything you can do," he said, not looking at her, "you'll have to do it soon."

Francie studied him. "Whose side are you on?" she asked. "I thought you wanted to bring it down."

"I don't know." He looked up when she didn't say anything. "That's the honest truth. If I was on the team that cut the biggest tree in the world it would be . . . well, at least then I would have done *something* big in my life, something everyone would remember. And people like your father are saying that all the extra lumber would save the company and help lift this depression. That'd be a good thing." He shoved his hands in his pockets. "But when I think about you and Carrie . . ." He sighed. "I'm not sure that's how I want to be remembered after all." He scuffed his boot back and forth, drawing an invisible line on the porch floor. "But I guess you didn't come up with anything." He looked at her. "Besides writing Mr. Court."

Francie shook her head. "If only I could prove some-how that the tree really did belong to Carrie they couldn't cut it, could they?" She shrugged. "But to prove that I'd need the will. And who knows where that is."

"Probably burned up in the cabin," Charlie agreed. "If there really was a will."

Francie closed her hands into fists. "There was a will. I know there was. Why would Carrie write in her diary that she'd seen it if she hadn't?"

Charlie shrugged. "But who knows if it was a legal will."

"She said it looked official. 'He showed me the will and it looks very official.' That's what she wrote."

"How would Carrie know what looked official or not?"

Francie knew he was right—Carrie wouldn't know what a legal will looked like. But an idea was beginning to grow in her mind.

"If Old Robert did have a will, where would he have put it, do you think?"

Charlie sat down on the porch swing, and Francie sat beside him. "In a box? On a shelf? Did Carrie mention anything about a box?"

Francie closed her eyes, trying to remember. "She said he kept two books on a corner shelf—the Bible and Shakespeare's sonnets. Nothing about a box. But she said one day he showed up in a suit that she thought he must have had put away somewhere. There was probably a chest for his clothes."

"That sounds right," Charlie agreed. "He would have kept anything valuable there, too."

"And that means it would have been burned up in the fire," Francie said. She brought her fist down hard on the swing's wide armrest. "If I were going to hide something, I'd put it where it wouldn't burn."

"Now you would," Charlie added. "Maybe he buried it."

Francie looked at him. The light from inside the house shone out and lit his face dimly. "If he buried it, it might still be there," she said slowly.

Charlie shook his head. "He could have buried it anywhere! You'd have to dig up half an acre and even then you might not find it."

But Francie refused to be discouraged. "It's worth a try. If I could find the will, I could save the tree. I know it!" She stood up. "I'll go tomorrow. Early. I'll look until I find it."

Charlie put a hand on her arm. "Your parents will never let you go there. It's too close to where we're logging."

"They won't know where I've gone. I'll figure out something. I don't care if I get in trouble, if they never let me go to the woods again in my life. If I can save Carrie's tree, I don't care what happens afterward."

"Well," he said, giving her shoulders a little shake. "Just be careful. Don't do anything dangerous. Promise me?"

Francie bit her lip and didn't answer him.

Charlie dropped his hands. "If you don't promise, I'll have to tell Uncle James." His face looked white and strained.

Finally Francie nodded. "I promise," she said. "Nothing dangerous."

Charlie nodded, satisfied. He gave her a quick kiss on the cheek, then clomped down the steps and out into the dark street.

Francie watched him go. She'd promised, but if she had to break this promise, she would. Carrie's promise came first. *I am the knight, sworn to protect my Emperor or die in the attempt.* Carrie had sworn. She wasn't here to keep that promise, but Francie was. She would keep Carrie's promise. No matter what.

· Chapter Fifteen ·

Stars were still gleaming in a navy blue sky when Francie slipped out of the house the next morning. She shivered in the damp predawn air. Her old wool sweater wasn't really warm enough now, but more outer clothing would only slow her down. She knew that she'd warm up as soon as she started walking. As silent as a shadow, she tiptoed around back to the shed where her father kept his tools. It was too dark to see inside the shed, but the long-handled shovel was always kept hanging on two nails by the door. Francie felt along the wall, and in a moment, her fingers wrapped around the smooth wood. Without a sound, she lifted it down. Hopefully, she thought, she'd have returned it before her father even missed it. The shed door creaked as she closed it, but her parents' room was on the other side of the house. They'd never hear such a small sound.

The street was deserted—not even the mill workers were up this early. She swung the shovel over her shoulder, crossed the street, and climbed the slope of the hill behind the hotel to the road. She figured it would take more than an hour to walk to Old Robert's cabin and she wasn't taking any chances of meeting loggers, or anyone else, on the path. By the time she got to the cabin, there would be enough light to search. If she were very lucky, she might find the will and be back to town before her mother missed her.

Francie had been in Connor's Basin alone many times, but the combination of dark and quiet she found there so early in the morning felt threatening, as if she had no business in this wild place. The sequoia stumps loomed above her like unfriendly giants, and Francie found herself wondering about bears. "I've never seen one here before," she said aloud, knowing that if he heard her voice, a bear would move off in another direction. Bears didn't want to meet up with humans any more than humans wanted to meet up with bears. She began reciting the Declaration of Independence and then the Preamble to the Constitution as she walked. "I wonder," she said, giggling suddenly, "how often the bears have to listen to the Preamble to the Constitution."

By the time she'd recited it ten times slowly, she had crossed Connor's Basin. In the four days since she'd found Carrie's tree, the almost invisible path that she and Charlie had followed into the woods at the north end of the basin had become a mud-slicked highway. "They must have brought the machinery up this way," she said, and then bit her lip at the loudness of her voice in the still forest. She didn't know exactly where the logging camp was, probably over on the other side of Connor's Pass, but it was time to start being quieter. Hopefully, the bears would be foraging somewhere else.

Loggers had chopped down trees and torn up the brambles—the path was now a ten-foot-wide track with the wood trash piled on either side. "At least I won't lose my way," she muttered, "even in the dark." But the incline was steep and even more slippery than it had been on Sunday. Francie moved off the path and walked beside it on the soft pine needles.

The light was growing, and sooner than she expected, she saw the dogwood still blooming off to her left where Old Robert's cabin had been. And just as she glimpsed the white blossoms, the *chug, chug* of the steam-powered donkey engine echoed faintly in the still air, getting ready to lower the cut logs down the skidroad to the mill. Work had begun at Carrie's tree. The logging camp must be farther up the mountain, Francie thought, for if it were anywhere around here, she would surely have seen some of the men on the path.

All the flowers were still blooming at the cabin site—the contrast between the fragile pink phlox and the burned and blackened logs made Francie's throat close up. Had Old Robert died here? Had he known what was happening? She felt a shiver up her spine. "Of course not," she said aloud, trying to banish the sense of "not right" she felt around the cabin.

It didn't help, but she forced herself to ignore the feelings. "I'm looking for your will," she informed any ghost who happened to be lurking around. "This is something you would want!"

But instead of stepping into the perimeter of logs that marked the cabin, she sat on an old stump and looked around. "Where did you hide your will?" she asked the ghost. Then she laughed. Charlie would think she'd gone crazy—talking to the air and thinking about ghosts. She wished he were here with her. Or Carrie. Carrie would know where Old Robert had hidden his will.

"The chimney was there," she said, pointing to the pile of vine-covered rocks, "and the cabin door was probably opposite it, here." She stood in front of the spot, trying to see a fully built cabin in her mind, imagining bunk beds against the wall, a table in the corner, and a trunk. "There might have been a front stoop, here." She pointed. "Would he bury a box by the front stoop?"

Not likely. She walked around the burned logs to the fallen chimney. This would have been the most likely place to bury a strongbox of valuables, Francie thought. The chimney would be the most durable part of the cabin.

When nothing else was left of a cabin site, the chimney usually survived as a visible marker.

"In fact," she said aloud, her excitement climbing, "if I were going to bury something, I'd bury it inside the cabin. After all, it had a dirt floor." She took a breath, stepped over the timbers, and stood in the middle of the cabin facing the chimney. "Right or left?" she asked herself.

"Right," she answered immediately. She placed the point of her shovel in the ground to the right of the pile of stones and began digging. But twenty minutes later she'd dug a hole a foot deep and a yard square without finding so much as a metal nail for her troubles, much less a box. She sighed and began on the left side.

But the result was the same. No box. She leaned her shovel against the pile of stones and straightened her stiff back. Maybe she wasn't digging deep enough, or maybe it was buried in a different place altogether. She glanced around. Charlie had been right—it would take weeks to dig up the whole cabin site. And what if Old Robert hadn't buried the will?

She tried to gauge the time from the sky. The sun was still hidden by trees, but the sky was lightening. If it had taken an hour to walk to the cabin and an hour to dig those holes—she glared down at them—then it might be as late as six thirty. "Mama is up by now," she said, but knew her mother wouldn't be concerned at her absence. It wasn't that unusual for Francie to go out early in the morning. Her mother wouldn't be happy about it, but she wouldn't worry. Not yet.

Francie pulled away a few of the vines and sat down on the edge of the pile of fallen chimney stones. "If he didn't bury the will," she said aloud, "where would he have hidden it?" Charlie had thought it would be in the trunk, but that must have burned up in the fire. And if the will had been burned up, then there was no point in looking for it now.

"But," Francie reasoned slowly, "if it's still here somewhere . . . if it didn't get burned up in the fire . . ." She let her glance roam around the cabin site. "It would be in some place that didn't burn."

"But the whole thing burned to the ground," she wailed, looking at all the blackened timbers. "There's nothing left."

And then she jumped up and stared at the fallen chimney. "Except the chimney," she whispered. And people did sometimes have hidey-holes in chimneys, didn't they? She grabbed at the vines that had overgrown the pile and in a short time had cleared them all away. Most of the stones were only about the size of a baby's head. She knelt in the dirt and began moving them, one at a time, piling them at her side. When her back felt as if it were burning with the effort to lift each stone, she stood up, stretched her hands up over her head, and then got back to work.

The stones got bigger as she got closer to the bottom of

the chimney. She had to use the shovel to pry them off the pile, watching each one clatter down and land in the dirt with a thump. She surveyed her work. She'd moved more than half the stones away from the site, but no hidey-hole was to be found.

"How far down will I have to go?" She had lost track of time entirely; all her attention was focused on the stones. Pry one up. Push it off the pile. Move it away. Pry another one up. Push it off. Move it away. Pry, push, move. She felt as if she'd been moving stones all her life.

And then, just when she was about to give up, she found it. She had stuck her shovel tip between two of the biggest stones so far, and using all her strength, she pushed the front one off the pile. And there, under the other big stone, she saw a corner of something—a piece of yellowed oilskin. She maneuvered the shovel tip under the stone, pried it up, and there it was, a square oilskin packet tied with a leather thong. She stared at it, not quite believing her eyes. She knelt, and with shaking fingers, picked up the packet. The leather thong, old and dried, broke into pieces as she picked at the knot. "Please let this be it," she prayed, and lifted the flap.

There were two folded papers inside. Francie sat on the ground and withdrew them carefully, placing them in her lap. Then, holding her breath, she slowly unfolded the one on top. The ink was faded and the paper was stained brown in places. The crease marks made some of the writing impossible to read. But Francie could see that it was a deed to a parcel of land, made out in the name of Robert Lloyd Granger. The date on the deed was July 14, 1866, just a year after the end of the Civil War.

The other piece of paper was the will. The ink on this paper, too, was faded, and although some of the letters were now illegible, Francie could see that Robert Lloyd Granger had left his land, the same parcel listed in the deed, and all the timber and minerals on that land, to Mary Carolyn Cavanaugh on July 5, 1887. Two other men had signed the will: Thomas Ferry and William Butler. Francie touched her sister's name with the tip of her finger. "I forgot she was named after Mama," she whispered, blinking back tears. She wiped her wet cheeks with the back of her hand and scrubbed them dry on her dress. Even a few drops of water might disintegrate this ancient paper. She folded the will and the deed back into their original shapes and slipped them into the oilskin pouch.

It wasn't until she was standing up that she realized that Old Robert's full name was Robert Lloyd Granger. *Granger!* Was he a relative of Lewis Granger, the manager of the lumber company? Francie looked north as if she might be able to see the logging going on around Carrie's tree. Was Robert Granger the father of Lewis Granger? Or his brother?

Without conscious thought, Francie found herself walking. It was getting late, she argued with herself. Mama will be worried. Father will be furious. She walked back to the path, but instead of turning south toward town, she turned north toward Carrie's tree. If Lewis Granger were the son or brother of Old Robert, then he would know about the will. He would know if it were legal. She had to talk to Lewis Granger, no matter what the consequences.

· Chapter Sixteen ·

A s she walked north, the sounds got louder: the chugging donkey engine, the whacks of the axes as they bit into the tree trunks, the shouts of the loggers. She let the noise of the logging drown out the warning voice in her head. *If Granger knows about the will, then he knows the lumber company is cutting illegally on Old Robert's land—on Carrie's land. And he won't want anyone reminding him of that—especially not Carrie's sister.*

She remembered when she'd met him in Connor's Basin that day and how strange he had acted. "He's a mean one," Charlie had said. But she shook that voice away as well. "If I show him the will," she told herself, "surely he'll stop the logging. He won't have a choice. Will he?" She didn't answer the question.

The land sloped precipitously up toward the pass, and she forced herself to walk faster. The noise was intense, but so far, she hadn't seen any evidence of logging, only the trampled road where they had moved the equipment. The trees still stood tall, crowding out the sunlight.

But as she reached the top of the pass and looked down into the opposite valley, she saw that here the world had changed. On Sunday there had been peace in this place. Birds called to each other. Squirrels chattered. The trees had been so tall and close together that they had blocked out the sunlight. The forest floor had been covered with a soft carpet of old roots and pine needles.

Now the place looked like the aftermath of a hurricane. Naked tree trunks lay all tumbled on the hillsides; some had fractured as they fell, some had been dynamited into more manageable pieces. The forest floor had been chopped and carved by the weight of the fallen trees chained together and dragged down the skidroad to the chute and then on down the mountain to the mill.

Carrie's tree was still untouched, but where on Sunday it had been surrounded by a thick forest, now it stood alone amid a rubble of wood chips and twisted branches. The loggers had gathered brush and the willowy trunks of saplings into an enormous pile that stretched out from the base of the sequoia—it looked like a kind of shaggy shadow of the tree. This was what the loggers called the featherbed—they hoped it would cushion the tree when it hit the earth and stop it from shattering. It worked, some-times.

Francie clenched her fists, trying to ignore the sadness that threatened to overwhelm her. "Look for Granger," she told herself. "He's the one who can stop this." She scanned the valley, searching among the busy figures for his strange ape-shaped body and balding head.

She saw him at the same time that he saw her—he shook the shoulder of the man he was speaking with and then pointed up to where she was standing. He was close enough that she could read the expression on his face—he certainly wasn't happy to see her there.

Well, she thought, I didn't expect him to be happy. She took a few steps down the path into the valley and looked at Granger again. He was holding up his hand, motioning her to stop. She did, and he went back to his conversation—obviously something about the giant train of logs they were getting ready to send down the chute.

Francie waited a few moments and then realized that Granger wasn't going to come up to speak to her. He just didn't want her in the valley. "Well," she said, "that's just too bad." She headed down the path again.

A shout she could hear above the donkey engine made her look up. Granger was yelling at her and pointing back up to the pass. He wanted her to go back.

Francie watched him for a moment, but it was clear that he wasn't moving toward her. So she smiled politely at him and took another step forward.

That did it. His face turned dark with anger. He

jammed his hat onto his head and marched toward her, raising dust with each furious step he took. Francie imagined she could almost hear his feet pounding in the dirt.

"What do you think you're doing, Miss Cavanaugh?" Granger roared when he got close enough for her to hear. "Children are absolutely forbidden on the logging site." He grabbed her shoulders, spun her around, and shoved her back toward the pass. "You will leave immediately, and you can be sure that I will report this to your father."

Francie stumbled a few steps up the path before she could stop herself. Then she whirled back to face him, as furious as he. "This land doesn't belong to the lumber company," she shouted back at him. "It belongs to us, and if you don't get your men off our land immediately, I'm going to call the sheriff!" She heard her own words as if they'd been spoken by someone else, and bit her lip. Now she was in for it. No well brought up young lady ever spoke like that!

Granger stared at her. Then he threw back his head and laughed. "How old are you, Miss Cavanaugh?" And his voice sounded almost kind.

Francie rubbed her shoulder where his fingers had gripped her hard enough to bruise. "Fifteen," she said. "But that doesn't matter. I—"

He interrupted her. "You go home to your parents and stop trying to meddle in affairs that don't concern you."

The noise from the logging had lessened somewhat.

Francie looked down and saw that some of the loggers had stopped their work to watch them. She closed her eyes, as the heat rose in her cheeks. *What am I doing? Father will be so angry.* But out of the corner of her eye, she saw that one of the loggers was Charlie, and somehow his presence gave her courage. She turned back to Granger. "This does concern me," she said more quietly. "I found the tree. If my father hadn't told you about it, you wouldn't be here now."

"That doesn't mean you own this land," Granger answered her with exaggerated patience.

"No, sir," said Francie, trying belatedly to be more polite, "but this does." She held up the tattered oilskin.

"And what is that," Granger said, as if he were talking to a very young child. He looked around at the loggers who were watching them, grinned, and shrugged as if he didn't know why he was wasting time talking to this youngster.

"It's a will," she said, stepping one more step away from him. "And the deed to this section of land." And she had the satisfaction of seeing Granger's superior expression fall into confusion.

"Where did you find that?" he growled. He was trying for the same haughty tone, but Francie could hear the sudden current of uncertainty in his voice.

"In the rubble of Old Robert's fireplace," she said, gesturing behind her in the direction of the burned cabin.

"The deed is made out to Robert Granger, and the will is in favor of Mary Carolyn Cavanaugh. My sister." She paused. "I think Robert Granger must be related to you," she added. "Is he?"

Granger took a step toward Francie. "Let me see that," he said, holding out his hand.

Francie saw Charlie's worried face as he glanced up at them. He began to move purposefully up the hill. She looked at Granger. Should she give him the will? Would he give it back to her?

"Robert Granger was my brother." Granger tried to grab the packet from her. "Give me those papers!" She stepped back, avoiding his hands, but she realized she didn't have any choice. He was an adult, and as he had pointed out, she was only a child. She took the deed out of the pouch and handed it to him but kept the will. "Old Robert must have gotten this land long before the lumber company was here," she said, noticing that Granger's hands unfolding the paper were not quite steady.

He read the deed in silence. Francie watched Charlie come up the path and stop about fifteen feet from where they were standing. He raised his eyebrows and Francie shook her head ever so slightly.

"This deed is no good," Granger said. "Let me see the will."

Francie felt her face go hot again. The words burst out of her. "How do you know it's no good?"

Granger's face turned almost purple. Spit foamed at the corners of his mouth. "Give me that will!" he sputtered. He lunged at Francie.

Francie spun around and took off running. She heard Granger's heavy breathing, almost like a growl, and the sudden exclamations of the loggers.

"Come back here!" Granger's voice was right behind her, his breath coming in gasps. She lifted her skirts with one hand, gripped the will tightly in the other hand, and sprinted up the hill.

"Run, Francie!" Charlie cheered her on. "You've got him!"

As she reached the pass, she glanced back. Charlie was waving. "We're starting to cut tomorrow!" he shouted.

Granger was still chasing her—she was only about twenty-five feet ahead of him. She raced across the flat saddle between the high peaks, and followed the path into the forest on the south side of the pass. It was downhill almost all the way into town now, she thought. That made it easier for her to run, but it would be easier for Granger, too. She could hear his pounding feet and ragged breaths, but she couldn't tell how far ahead she was, and she wouldn't take the time to look back.

"I wish I could take off my boots," she said between clenched teeth. But there wasn't time for that, either. She forced her legs to move even faster down the trail, past the dogwood that marked Old Robert's cabin. Now the track got steep and slippery. Francie veered off the path and ran almost silently in the pine needles beside it where there was less chance of slipping. The steep incline forced her to slow down, and she let her breath fall into the familiar rhythm. She could no longer hear Granger's feet or his harsh breathing. "But I can't stop," she said.

She was past the steepest part of the trail and running on the flat at the north end of Connor's Basin when she heard Granger's shout. Without meaning to, she glanced back. He was at least a quarter mile behind her, right at the steepest and slipperiest part of the track. Suddenly his feet flew out from underneath him and he fell. His shout turned into a high-pitched yell, almost a scream. For an instant, Francie stopped, watching him tumble over and over down the hill toward her.

"No!" she shouted aloud, and took off again. But she couldn't stop herself from looking back once more. In a quick glimpse, she thought she saw Granger pulling himself to his feet at the bottom of the hill. She faced forward and put on even more speed as she wove her way between the giant sequoia stumps in the basin. She didn't stop until she reached the road into town.

By this time Granger had been left far behind, she was sure of it. She leaned against a tree by the side of the road and let her breath return to normal. She glanced back now and then, but from the quiet she knew he was no longer following her. She looked at the oilskin packet in her hand.

Granger had the deed, but she still had the will.

She fingered it. Who would know if it were legal? Father?

"But I can't show it to him," she said. "What if he takes it back to Granger?"

Would Mrs. Mansfield, the would-be senator's wife, help her? "Not likely," she said, sniffing. She wouldn't defy her husband, any more than Francie's mother would defy Father. "Thank goodness I haven't got a husband yet," Francie whispered. She grinned ruefully. The way she'd been acting, it would be a long while before anyone would want to marry her!

What about Mr. Court? Francie folded her lips down into a thin line. A lot of help he'd been so far! He hadn't paid any attention to her letter anyway. "If he got it," Francie added, startling a robin that had just perched on the branch above her head. He flew off, chirping his "cheerio" call. Francie thought it sounded as if the bird were laughing at her.

She sighed and began the walk back to town, trying not to think of how angry her mother and father would be by now. "It must be almost noon," she said, searching the sky. But low clouds were now covering the sun—she couldn't tell what time it was.

"Tomorrow," she whispered. "Less than twenty-four hours." If only she could walk into Mr. Court's office in St. Joseph and plunk the will down on his desk. Then he'd have to do something.

"But how could I get to St. Joseph?" The stage didn't come until tomorrow—much too late. On horseback? It took most of a day to ride down the winding and sometimes treacherous road out of the mountains to St. Joseph, but Francie considered borrowing her father's mare and trying to make the trip. "I probably can't get in any more trouble than I'm in now," she said aloud. But then she remembered that the mare was lame. And borrowing anyone else's horse was truly unthinkable. "That would be stealing," she said, and not worth it, since the chances of getting to St. Joseph in time on horseback were slim, anyway.

If only she could jump on a bundle of boards and ride the flume down to St. Joseph, she thought. That would truly be the fastest way—riding the flume. She laughed out loud, imagining Charlie's face if she indeed rode the flume to St. Joseph.

What a crazy idea! She'd only heard of two men riding the flume successfully—those two last summer. They had been arrested as soon as they got to St. Joseph. Two others had tried before that. One had ended up in the hospital, and the other man had been killed—he'd fallen where the flume scaffolding was one hundred feet from the boulder-strewn hillside.

"But that man was drunk," Francie remembered. O'Brien and Murphy, the two who made it all the way to St. Joseph, were both small, wiry men, fast on their feet and with good balance. O'Brien was a wrestler—nobody had ever beaten him in a match. And Murphy always won the footraces held every Fourth of July.

"Charlie thought I could beat him," Francie said, thinking that she was also fast on her feet. And she had good balance, too. Carrie had said so in her diary. Her heart began to beat in slow, painful thuds. Was it such a crazy idea? Did she dare try it? Could she ride the flume to St. Joseph?

She glanced at the sky again and rubbed her shaking hand on her skirt. "Is there any other way to get there in time?" she asked herself. Not by horseback, and not by stagecoach. And certainly not walking—it was forty miles to St. Joseph.

Maybe someone else could go on horseback. She could send the will and a letter explaining everything. She held the oilskin pouch on her palm, and then clutched it to her. She couldn't trust it to anybody else. There was the telegraph office, but even if the operator would let her telegraph to Mr. Court—"Not likely," she grunted—what if Mr. Court ignored her telegram the way he'd ignored her letter? She needed to talk to him, face-to-face.

Thoughts spun around in Francie's head so fast she felt dizzy. Was riding the flume the only way to get to St. Joseph? Could she do it?

"They'd never let me near it," Francie whispered, knowing that the mill workers in Connorsville wouldn't let her even enter the yard. She imagined sneaking into the yard after dark, but she discarded the notion immediately. "The courthouse would be closed," she said, "and so would the newspaper office."

Somehow those thoughts calmed her. "It's impossible," she said, firmly tucking the pouch into the bodice of her dress. "Even if I could ride it, I won't have the chance."

She had begun walking back to town when she remembered Two Creek Mill. It had been abandoned years earlier when the loggers moved their operations to the opposite end of Connor's Basin. But at one time, Two Creek Mill had been the beginning of the flume line.

Francie's steps got slower, until she was standing absolutely still in the middle of the dirt road. "I'll just go look at it," she said. "I won't get on—I'll just look. There probably won't even be a flume boat there."

· Chapter Seventeen ·

B ut there was an old flume boat. In fact, there were two of them sitting beside the flume. The V-shaped track was close to the ground here, built low so the mill workers could slide the bundles of boards into the water without too much trouble. She shut out all thoughts and watched the clear water in the track swirl by—the day was warm and it looked as inviting as a cool mountain stream.

She placed one foot on the X-shaped trestle that formed the flume scaffolding, stepped up and put her hand into the water, cupping her palm to feel the strength of the current. The land here was flat, so the water tugged only gently on her fingers. On the mountainside's steep grades, however, she knew that the water ran faster than a steam locomotive.

"Don't think about that," Francie told herself, hopping down from the scaffolding. She bent down to examine the flume boats. They looked like animal drinking troughs with one end missing; they were V-shaped to fit into the flume. A flat board fit just inside the top of the V; that was the seat. Two narrow boards had been nailed crosswise across the top as extra protection to keep the contents of the boat from sliding out. She picked up the splintery end of one boat. It was heavy, but she raised it up about two feet and then dropped it—letting it thump down into the dirt. Then she sat in it, bracing her hips on one side and her feet on the other. She rocked back and forth, trying to push the two boards that formed the V-shape apart, but they held fast. The boat appeared perfectly sound.

Francie's cheeks were burning and her heart was pounding. She traced the outline of the pouch, hidden inside her bodice. Even if she got soaked, the oilskin would protect the will, she thought. "But the boat's too heavy. I can't even lift it up into the flume," she said aloud.

A sudden gurgle and splash to her right made her turn and look up as a bundle of lumber slid past her heading for St. Joseph. She imagined its trip to St. Joseph, floating down the flume just as logs float down a stream. It would be prodded and pushed by the flume herders, stationed in their little houses along the flume track. But once a load of lumber was put into the flume, not even the flume herders could stop it. She could feel her knees trembling, and she walked across the abandoned mill yard away from the flume. "I can't do it," she said. Her eyes filled with tears.

They would begin cutting Carrie's tree tomorrow and nobody would be there to stop them.

"If only there were another way!" She cried out and the sound of her voice came echoing back to her. "But there isn't," she whispered, and she heard no echo of that soft sound.

Biting her lip she turned back to the flume. "At least I should see if I can get that boat into the flume," she said. She gritted her teeth, grabbed the edge of the flume boat, and dragged it to the scaffolding. She lifted one end up until the boat stood with one end on the ground—the end in her hands just cleared the edge of the flume track. She hooked her fingers around the end of the boat that rested on the ground, and with a mighty heave, she pushed it up. It rose up in the air like a breaching whale, and then fell forward, resting cross-wise on the flume. The water rushed under it on its way to St. Joseph.

"I did it!" A rush of pride pushed away her fears. An image of her father's face crowded into her mind, but she forced it away. "Think only of riding this boat," she said, wondering if it would buck like an unbroken horse. Well, she had ridden an unbroken horse once, if it came to that. She and Carrie and Charlie had tried to ride Father's mare before she'd been broken to the saddle. Carrie had borne the brunt of the punishment for that adventure, she remembered. But Francie had stayed on the horse the longest.

She climbed up onto the flume and moved the boat until it was just inches from sliding into the flume. "Please let me be able to hold it," she prayed, and nudged the boat into the water.

Her prayer was answered. The boat lurched like an impatient pony, but the current was slow here, and Francie could hold it with one hand. "Please, let my father forgive me when he finds out," she prayed again. Holding the boat with one hand and the side of the flume with the other, she eased herself onto the flat board seat. Then, taking a deep breath, she let go of the flume track and grabbed the narrow piece of wood in front of her. The water slapped the back of the boat, and it moved off down the flume.

At first it was like floating on a raft down a lazy river. The flume was no more than four or five feet from the ground, and Francie's perch was above the level of the water. The water swirled around the boat, gurgling peacefully. Francie leaned forward, shifting to her knees, and the boat bobbed down, then up again. She heard the grating sound of wood scraping against wood, but her momentum did not slow.

In fact, as the flume track headed down the mountainside, the pace of the little boat increased. Francie gasped the first time cold water splashed in over the back of the boat, wetting her up to her waist. Her fingers gripped the wooden crosspiece, and she hunkered down, determined to hold on no matter what.

As the mountainside became steeper, the scaffolding upon which the flume was built became higher. It was as if the little boat were rising up into the air. Now Francie was level with the tops of the trees—she felt like a bird flying through the forest. If she let go . . . if she held out her arms . . . but instead she grabbed the crossbar even more tightly.

Water splashed up in front like a geyser, drenching her from head to foot. She could hardly breathe—she squeezed her eyes shut and leaned forward, blocking the onslaught of water just enough to grab a breath of air.

She had no idea how fast she was going, but everything she fixed her gaze on whisked out of her vision as fast as it came into it—trees, rocks, outcroppings all went by in a green-and-brown blur. When she looked ahead, the flume track was heading straight down. It was impossible that the boat could stay on the track. "We're going to fall," she cried, curling herself into the smallest possible ball over the crossbar. She made her mind a blank and let the water stream over her back.

Then the momentum slowed a bit. Francie sat up carefully, feeling the boat bob and lurch as it bounced from one side of the track to the other. She glanced back once, but the sight of the steep grade she'd just come down made her almost nauseated. She looked forward and did not turn around again.

Looming ahead was the first flume house. Francie had

thought her heart could not beat any harder without exploding, but she was wrong. Now she thought she could hear it beating over the waterfall noise of the water. She blinked against the splashing water and looked for the herder. He wasn't at his post beside the flume; instead, he was sitting on his little porch, leaning back in a chair with his hat tipped over his eyes. "Please don't let him see me," she murmured as the boat flew by—but she didn't dare look back to find out.

She was getting used to the furious pace and the continual flow of water over and around her. Her knees were beginning to ache from kneeling in one position for so long, but there was nothing she could do to ease them—if she sat down she wouldn't be able to balance as well. How long had she been traveling? How much farther would it be? She clenched her teeth together—she would just have to bear it.

And then, suddenly, there was no more water. Wood screeched against wood and the flume boat stopped. She lost her grip on the crossbar and was flung the full length of the boat. She opened her eyes to find that she had overrun the water. She scrambled back to her knees and just had time to grab the crossbar before the water came tumbling after her, slapping the flat rear of the boat and jerking her forward.

There was little time to think, but she realized how lucky she'd been. If she had been sitting down, or if the grade she'd been traveling had been much steeper, she might have been thrown out altogether. "I wonder if that's what happened to the man who died," she said. She peered over the side of the boat, watching the ground fall away below her. She was coming to the river, and Francie knew that this was where the flume rode farthest above the ground—to a height of almost one hundred feet. She checked to make sure she was in the center of the boat and held on tight. If the boat stopped again, she must be ready. She couldn't count on being lucky another time.

The boat rounded a bend and Francie could see another flume house ahead. She didn't know how close together the houses were, but there must be more herders to pass before she got to St. Joseph. She couldn't possibly hope to get by all of them without being seen. She hunkered down as she'd done before, but this herder was standing on a platform beside the flume. She heard him shout as she sped by.

"But I can't stop," she murmured. "And I don't see how he can stop me."

She was getting the hang of riding the flume. Each time the boat slowed, she rose up and leaned over the crossbar to give her knees a rest. When the boat gathered speed, she crouched low and moved with the rhythm of the water as it bobbed along. It reminded her a little of running.

At the next flume house, the herder was standing on the platform. As she approached, she could tell he was expecting her—he had his long, curved picaroon held up and looked like he was going to try to hook her as she went by. "I'll be stabbed," she cried, and tried to scoot to the far side of the boat. He leaned forward, but at the last moment raised the hook as she whisked by. She heard him call out and saw his angry brows and his mouth twisted in a shout, but there wasn't anything she could do. She couldn't stop, either.

How had he known she was coming? And then she remembered that each house was equipped with one of those newfangled telephone devices. It was one of the innovations Thomas Connor always bragged about. None of the houses or businesses in the mountains had telephones, but Connor had run lines to the flume houses so that each herder could telephone to the next. Of course they knew she was coming!

At the next house the herder was standing on the platform, but he only watched her. And at the next, the man cheered. "You're going to make it, girlie," he shouted, grinning. "Not far now." She was afraid to let go of the crossbar, but she smiled at him as she went by. They were letting her go, she thought, amazed. They thought she was doing it for fun.

She was out of the mountains when the boat overshot the water again and stopped once more. She glanced back to see that the stream of water was only a trickle. Ahead was the town of St. Joseph—she could see the buildings in the distance. It couldn't be more than a mile away now. She thought about the herders calling, letting the people in the mill yard know she was coming. They'd be waiting at the end of the line to cheer her. Or maybe to arrest her.

She knew what she had to do. She grabbed the side of the flume and swung over, first one leg and then another until she was standing on the narrow ledge the herders used. Her clothes were soaking wet and her fingers were numb, but she was only about twenty feet from the ground here, and she climbed down easily. It wouldn't take very long to walk to St. Joseph. They were expecting her to arrive on the flume boat, and they thought she was trying to make the ride all the way into town. They wouldn't start looking for her until the empty boat floated into the mill yard.

· Chapter Eighteen ·

The hot valley sun had begun to dry Francie's clothes by the time she made it to town. She took her time, walking slowly at first until her cramped legs loosened and warmed. Her boots were soaked and felt as if they were rubbing her feet raw, but that couldn't be helped. She would have plenty of time to sit down later. She walked beside the flume scaffolding for a while, but when she could see the road, she crossed the rough, open land and finished the journey that way. Following the flume would lead her straight to the finishing mill and into the arms of the sheriff!

St. Joseph's Main Street was, as usual, teaming with people. Francie's stomach was growling and she was beginning to feel weak from hunger. She'd had nothing to eat since before dawn this morning.

Mouth watering, she stopped to look in the window of

a baker's shop, but she had no money to buy food. For the first time in what seemed like hours, she thought about her parents. They were probably frantic with worry, even if they'd heard she'd been seen riding the flume. Especially if they heard that. She sighed and moved on.

The offices of the *St. Joseph Herald* were not on Main—Francie found that out by walking the whole length of the street and halfway back again. Finally she stopped into the hardware store.

She made her way through stacks of crates and barrels of nails to the counter, smoothing her damp hair back with her fingers and trying to ignore the curious look the clerk gave her. "Can you tell me where the office of the *St. Joseph Herald* is?"

His eyes widened. He was young, almost as young as she was herself. "Were you in an accident?" he asked her.

She looked down at her skirt, streaked with dirt and torn at the hem. "Sort of," she answered. "If you could tell me where the newspaper office is?"

"I'll show you," he said, his eyes narrowing with concern. He led her back out onto the wooden sidewalk in front of the store. "Go to the next side street and turn left—it's two blocks on the right."

The newspaper offices were on the second floor. Francie could hear the clacking of the big press and voices calling to one another as she climbed the stairs. She felt as if she had lead weights tied to her feet—she could barely make the effort to lift her foot to the next step. She wondered suddenly what she would do if Mr. Court wasn't in, or if he wouldn't see her. "If he won't talk to me about the sequoias," she said, "maybe he'll want a story about riding the flume." She knew that some day she might be proud of what she'd done, but right now all she felt was numb and discouraged. She pushed open the door—it had one frosted glass window and "St. Joseph Herald Offices" in black letters on the front—and went in.

She was immediately swallowed up in the noise. On her left was the pressroom. The floor vibrated with the clatter of the long press—its cylinders were turning and seemingly endless sheets of paper were whipping under them. Through the half-opened door she could see men in ink-smudged aprons pacing around the machine. They were shouting at each other, and Francie couldn't tell if they were angry or excited. A linotype machine nearly filled the small middle room—another man in an even dirtier apron was studying a piece of paper pinned to a board on his right, and he was tapping on the keyboard without looking at it. On the right was a closed door with a frosted window like the one through which she'd already passed. "Franklin Court—Editor" was printed there in thick black letters. Francie knocked softly, and when she heard no answer, turned the handle and pushed the door open.

"Can I help you?" The woman at the desk spoke before she looked up. She had dark brown hair caught up in long braids that wrapped around her head so many times she looked as if she were wearing a crown.

"May I see Mr. Court, please?" asked Francie, shutting the door on the noisy rooms behind her. Hunger was beginning to make her feel weak. If she could only hold up until she saw Mr. Court.

"Whom shall I say . . ." The woman's voice faded into silence as she looked up and took in Francie's dirty face and torn skirt. "What happened?" she asked, springing to her feet. "Are you all right?"

Francie grabbed the corner of the desk to keep herself from falling. "I need to speak with Mr. Court," she said, but the words came out in a whisper. "I'm Frances Cavanaugh."

The woman had come around the front of the desk. She took Francie by the elbow and half led, half carried her to the nearest chair. "Sit here," she said. "You look awful."

"I . . ." Francie's head was spinning. How could she explain the last few hours? "What time is it?"

The woman glanced at the grandfather clock standing by the door. "Not quite two o'clock," she said.

"I think I'm just hungry," Francie said. She tried to speak in her normal voice, but it came out just above a whisper. "I haven't eaten since dawn, and I've . . ."

"You've been in some kind of accident." The woman smoothed Francie's tangled hair. "Wait there."

She disappeared into the next room but came back

almost immediately with a glass of milk and a small brown bun. "Here," she said, putting the food down on a small table in front of Francie's chair. "You eat. Mr. Court has been called out to cover a story, but he'll be back soon. I'm sure he'll want to talk to you. Whatever has happened to you, it certainly looks like news!"

Francie ate the bun in silence—it was made of coarse flour and had raisins scattered through it. The woman had gone back to her desk and was typing something on a shiny new typewriter. The noise from the other rooms reached here only faintly; Francie rested her head on the paneled wall behind her and closed her eyes.

The slam of the door jerked her awake. Mr. Court came bursting into the room like a tornado. "Damn and blast," he shouted, throwing his coat in the direction of the coat-rack in the corner. "That girl didn't show up! Hurst, the last flume herder, telephoned when she passed his station, but the boat came in empty. After half an hour the sheriff sent out a party on horseback to search." He dug in his trouser pockets and came up with a handful of paper scraps, which he dumped onto his secretary's desk. "We can't hold up the evening edition much longer, but I don't want to go to press without this story! Miss Jordan, we'll give Sheriff Bennett half an hour. If we haven't heard anything by then, I'll walk over to the jail to see what's up."

Miss Jordan had risen when he came through the door. Now she put a hand on his arm, stopping him as he was heading to a closed door behind her desk. This door did not have a window and was marked "F. Court—Private." Miss Jordan nodded toward Francie. "This young woman has been waiting for you, Mr. Court."

He swung around and stared at Francie, taking in her torn and dirty clothes and her tangled hair.

Francie jumped up. "I'm Francie Cavanaugh," she said. "I need to talk to you about—"

"You're the young woman who rode the flume this morning." His eyes seemed to bore into her as if he were testing her strength. Then his lip quirked up into what might have been a smile. "I'm glad to find you safe. How did you get here?" He motioned her to sit and pulled up another chair to sit beside her. She half expected him to pull out a tablet of paper and begin taking notes. He didn't, but she got the feeling he was remembering every word she said.

"I was afraid the sheriff would be waiting for me. I couldn't let him arrest me, not before I'd talked to you. So I left the flume before the boat came to town."

Mr. Court raised his eyebrows and sat back in his chair. "Usually it's the newspaperman who goes looking for the story. Not the story that comes to the newspaperman. Surely you knew I'd be waiting to interview you when you came into the lumberyard. How could I resist? A woman riding the flume—that's news!"

Francie clasped her hands together so tightly her fingers

turned white. "It's not riding the flume I want to talk to you about—it's about cutting down Carrie's sequoia. Did you get my letter? Can you help?"

Mr. Court hit his forehead with the palm of his hand, and then laughed out loud. "Frances Cavanaugh! I knew you seemed familiar. You're the girl who was going to count the rings of that old sequoia stump for me. I did get your letter, but I was in San Francisco until yesterday afternoon. I only saw it last night when I stopped in the office on my way home." He crossed one ankle over the other knee, brushing invisible lint off his immaculate trousers. "You'd better begin at the beginning."

So Francie told him everything, from finding Carrie's note in the knothole of the stump to her wild ride down the flume to St. Joseph. "It was the only way I could get here fast enough," she said.

"You did bring the will with you, didn't you?" Mr. Court asked, looking around.

Francie felt herself blush, but she reached inside the bodice of her shirtwaist and pulled out the oilskin pouch. She took out the will and handed it to Mr. Court.

He unfolded it in silence. He looked at it for a long moment, and Francie could see his eyes following the lines of print across the page. He turned it over and then held it up to the light. "It certainly looks genuine," he admitted. "But I'll take it over to the land office. They'll have the deed on record." He looked up, not at Francie, but past her, as if he could see something on the wall behind her. She had to fight the temptation to turn her head to see what he was looking at.

"What I don't understand," he murmured, "is how the lumber company could have a deed to this land if it belongs to Robert Granger." Then he came to his feet as suddenly as if he were a jack-in-the-box on a spring. "That question can be answered quickly enough." He grabbed his coat and shrugged his arms into the sleeves. "Never mind the sheriff, Miss Jordan. Just take down Miss Cavanaugh's story for the evening edition." He turned to Francie. "Repeat what you told me," he said. "I'm going to the land office and the courthouse." He put his hand on the door and then turned back. "I'll telegraph to your parents, too, and let them know you're safe." He pointed at Miss Jordan. "And see if you can find Miss Cavanaugh some clean clothes." And he was gone.

Telling her story to Miss Jordan was easier than telling it to Mr. Court—Miss Jordan nodded and smiled, making her feel as if everything she said made perfect sense.

"Now you'll want those clean clothes," Miss Jordan said when she'd finished. "If you'll wait here, I think I can find some for you."

Too tired now for more conversation, Francie only nodded. Miss Jordan patted her shoulder and left the room.

She was back in less than fifteen minutes with some clothes draped over her arm. "These belong to my niece—

she's not quite as tall as you are, but she lives just two blocks away," she said, handing Francie a soft skirt of a dark green wool and a crisp white shirtwaist, along with lace-trimmed drawers, a camisole, and a white petticoat decorated with little pink ribbons. She looked down at Francie's feet doubtfully. "But I don't think I can find shoes in your size."

Francie lifted up one foot. "My boots are almost dry," she said. "And so are my stockings."

Miss Jordan smiled, and led her into Mr. Court's private office. "Do you need any help dressing?"

Francie shook her head. "No, thank you," she said. And Miss Jordan left, closing the door behind her.

Francie stood in the middle of the room, clutching the clothes. The office was paneled in a dark wood, and the library table that Mr. Court must use for a desk matched it. On the table was a huge dictionary and some other books, flanked with brass bookends in the shape of books. A pile of blank sheets of paper, a number of pens, a big bottle of ink and a blotter were all neatly arranged in the center. This must be where Mr. Court wrote his articles. A stone fireplace took up most of one wall, and on another wall there was one window overlooking the street.

Francie stood as far from the window as she could get. She took off her sweater and unbuttoned her shirtwaist and skirt. It felt wonderful to step out of her dirty clothes, still damp from the flume ride. She slipped on the drawers and camisole and adjusted the petticoat. She pulled the white shirtwaist over her head without unbuttoning it, and slipped into the wool skirt. It was a bit too short, but it fit in the waist. She ran her fingers through her tangled hair, wondering what her mother would think if she knew her daughter was changing clothes in the newspaper office. She didn't have to wonder what her father would think—she shuddered and hoped he would never learn of it. She smoothed her skirt and went back to the waiting area.

"Could I borrow some pins for my hair?" she asked Miss Jordan.

"Certainly," she said. She opened a drawer in her desk and picked out a comb and some pins, handing them to Francie with a smile.

"Thank you," Francie said. She sat down and quickly twisted her hair up the way Carrie had worn hers. Nobody in St. Joseph would mind—they didn't even know Carrie here.

It must not have been very difficult to find out what Mr. Court wanted to know—he was back shortly after Francie settled herself in her chair. This time he came in quietly. He nodded to Francie but, without a word, he went into his office and shut the door. Francie looked at Miss Jordan, who shrugged. "He's often like that," she said. "He's figuring something out."

Soon he called through the door. "Send Miss Cavanaugh in here."

Francie went in. Mr. Court was sitting in the big wooden armchair by the table, staring at the will, which he'd smoothed out flat on the table. But he rose when Francie entered the room. He motioned for her to sit down in one of the large stuffed chairs by the fireplace. He picked up the will and sat down across from her.

"Well, I found the answer," Mr. Court said. "Or part of it, anyway." He nodded. "The deed is genuine. Though most of the land around Connorsville wasn't put up for sale until it was surveyed, a few people, like Robert Granger, staked out claims before that. So this land apparently does belong to Robert Granger and not the Sierra Lumber Company." He raised his eyebrows and tapped at the paper with his finger. "Quite an error on their part," he said, "though if the man's dead, and the documents hadn't come to light, who would have known the difference?" He shook his head.

Francie rubbed her fingers back and forth on the thick velvet pile of the chair. "Is the will . . . could you check?"

Mr. Court nodded. "The will is perfectly genuine. William Butler has left the law firm—it's simply Ferry and Sons now. But Thomas Ferry remembers old Robert Granger clearly. It was the only time he'd come to the office and the will was straightforward enough." He rubbed his chin with his hand. "At the time Ferry didn't realize the land Granger was willing to your sister was supposedly lumber company land, or he'd have put in an inquiry." He looked at Francie. "But your sister . . ." he paused, a frown creasing his forehead. He was obviously wondering how to put it delicately.

Francie helped him out. "She's dead. She died in an accident in the mountains six years ago."

Mr. Court nodded. "So that means, I suppose, that the land passes to your father. Unless your sister made a will."

Francie shook her head. "I don't think she did."

Mr. Court folded the will and handed it to Francie. "From what you said in your letter, I assume you'd like to try to use this information to stop Granger from cutting down that tree."

Francie nodded. "It's possible isn't it? He can't cut the tree if it doesn't belong to him, can he?"

"Not legally," he said. "Unless he were given permission from the owner. Or the company could offer to buy the land or the timber rights." He paused, as if he were again thinking about how to express his thought. "When I was visiting last spring, I got the feeling that your father would not be against cutting this tree. Am I right? He would likely give his permission?"

Francie nodded, feeling the tears fill her eyes. She blinked and looked away from Mr. Court's gentle gaze. "I guess it's not worth trying," she whispered.

Mr. Court cleared his throat. "Well, I wouldn't say that." He leaned forward. "I'm against the logging. You know that already." He looked up at Francie and smiled when she nodded. "I'm ready to give those folks just as much trouble as I can. If we can't stop them, we can at least embarrass them, and maybe hold them up a little. Time is money for these fellows. Do you understand?"

Francie nodded. She ran her fingers under her eyes, wiping away the tears, and tried to calm the sudden leap of hope in her chest. "But they're going to start cutting tomorrow."

"Tomorrow!" He whistled. "That doesn't give us much time, does it." He looked at her with new respect in his eyes. "No wonder you chose to ride the flume here. I must admit, Miss Cavanaugh, when you appeared here at my office I thought . . ." He cleared his throat. "Well, I thought you were just a kid out on a lark. Or one of those newshounds, looking for publicity." He looked at her again. "But now I think I understand."

He jumped up, reminding Francie again of a jack-in-the-box. "We've got to get going. It's a long ride back to Connorsville. I'd prefer not to travel that route at night, but it seems we've no other choice." He put his hands in his pockets and looked down at her. "I'll need some supper before we leave, and I'll wager you will, too."

· Chapter Nineteen ·

On the way out of town, they stopped at the jail. Sheriff Bennett must have been watching for them out his office window—no sooner did Mr. Court pull the horses to a stop than the sheriff was out the door and climbing into the backseat of the buggy beside Francie.

"This is Miss Frances Cavanaugh," said Mr. Court. "She's the girl who . . ."

But no explanations were needed. "So you're the girl who caused me so much trouble this afternoon," he said, looking her up and down as if he were figuring out what size cell to put her in. He was a big man with wild gray hair that stuck out from under his wide-brimmed hat. He was dressed all in black: black pants, black vest—even his shirt was black.

Mr. Court snapped the lines, and the horses started off at a trot.

"Yes, sir," Francie said. "I didn't mean to inconvenience you."

Sheriff Bennett put his head back and roared with laughter. "Inconvenience," he spluttered when he could get his breath. "Well, that's one way to put it. Eight men on the payroll for four hours . . . to say nothing of the worry. We thought you'd broken your neck and the coyotes had dragged off your body." He looked at her over the tops of his glasses.

"Are you going to arrest me?" she asked him in a small voice. What would her father say to that, she wondered, realizing she had already gone way beyond any trouble Carrie had ever caused.

"Well," Sheriff Bennett drawled. "That depends. I thought you'd done it for a lark." He tapped his finger on his thigh.

"No, sir," Francie broke in. "I wasn't. I . . ."

He held up his hand. "Court advised me of the real situation. And under the circumstances, I don't see how you could have done any different." He raised one finger. "Mind, I don't say you shouldn't have talked this over with your parents."

"But they never would have let me try it," Francie blurted out.

"A simple telegram could have started the process in motion," Sheriff Bennett said.

Francie fell silent, listening to the *clop-clopping* of the horses' hooves on the dirt road. It was true. If her father had sent a telegram to Mr. Court or Sheriff Bennett, they could have checked on the will and the deed. If . . .

"My father would not do anything to stop the logging," Francie's voice was low. "He disagrees with Mr. Court."

Sheriff Bennett nodded. "So Court tells me," he said. "So, as I said, under the circumstances, I don't think you'll be spending any time in jail. This time." He gave her a stern look, but Francie thought she could see the corners of his lips quivering, as if they wanted to turn up in a smile. "It's going to be a long night, Court. I'll sleep now if you don't mind."

The mountains in front of them were purple in the sunset, and the sky was streaked with orange and scarlet. Mr. Court kept the horses to a trot. They would make good time on the flat ground and even after they entered the rolling foothills, but before too long they would have to slow down—no horse could trot all the way to Connorsville over the narrow, rocky trail they'd be following, especially at night.

Mr. Court looked over his shoulder at Francie. "Why don't you try to get some sleep as well," he suggested.

The rocking motion of the buggy made Francie think of a cradle, but she knew she wouldn't be able to sleep. Her mind was filled with questions. What would happen when they got to Connorsville? Would Sheriff Bennett and Mr. Court be able to stop Lewis Granger from cutting down the tree? But the biggest question of all was what her father would say when they asked him what he wanted to do with the tree since it really belonged to him. And she already knew the answer to that one.

She closed her eyes, anyway, thinking she would be wise to do whatever Mr. Court and Sheriff Bennett told her to do. It would be hard enough to face her father with their support. If they saw her as a troublemaker, it would be even worse. She wrapped herself in the musty-smelling carriage blanket Mr. Court had handed her before they left, huddled in a corner of the buggy, and tried to sleep.

She awoke with a jolt as the buggy swayed violently, throwing her against Sheriff Bennett. She could hear Mr. Court swearing at the horses; his shape was a darker shadow against a dark sky as he leaned back, pulling on the lines to slow the horses to a stop.

"What the hell is going on?" shouted Sheriff Bennett as he and Francie struggled to untangle themselves. One side of the buggy seat seemed to be dragging on the ground.

"Lost a wheel," Mr. Court said, and then, "Easy, Sam, easy, Jim," to the horses. He climbed down from the buggy and turned to help Francie and then the sheriff out as well.

The three of them stood in the darkness and surveyed the damage. "Doesn't look too bad," Sheriff Bennett commented. "The shaft's still whole, at any rate." He looked around him and whistled. "We're lucky we didn't go off the cliff, though."

The wheels of the buggy were less than a yard from the side of the road, a narrow track, which seemed to have been carved out of the solid rock of the mountain—it skirted the edge of a precipitous drop straight into the valley far below. This trail wound its way to a pass almost at the top of the first range, and then descended in the same kind of shelf road into Connorsville. Francie's heart seemed to drop into her stomach as she looked down into the darkness of the valley. If they'd gone off, they'd all have been killed.

Slowly she backed away from the edge. Sheriff Bennett and Mr. Court were unhitching the horses. "Miss Cavanaugh," Mr. Court called to her. "Can you walk down the trail a bit and see if you can find the wheel? If it's not busted, I think Sheriff Bennett and I could get it back on."

Francie nodded. The moon was half full and gave enough light to see by. Francie followed the trail, staying as far away from the edge as she could. About a quarter mile down she found the wheel, leaning up against a large rock that was half buried in the middle of the path. She stood the wheel on end and tested each spoke—they all seemed sound. "I've got it," she called back to the men, and then, with both hands, she rolled the wheel back up the hill to the buggy.

"Good girl," Sheriff Bennett said, taking the wheel from her. "Now, can you hold the horses while Court and I see if we can repair this thing?"

The horses, Sam and Jim, had calmed and were watching the proceedings with eyes big and almost liquid in the moonlight. "Hey, fellow," Francie whispered, rubbing her hand down Sam's forehead and then over his soft, soft nose. He blew a gentle breath out into her palm and nibbled on her fingers. Jim stamped his foot and gave a prodigious sigh.

"I hope they get it fixed, too." Francie kept her voice low so as not to startle them. She kept hold of the hitching straps Mr. Court had attached to the horses' bridles but moved off a few paces to sit on a large boulder. Sam and Jim lowered their heads, sniffing for what little green there might be on the rocky hillside.

The repair took two hours, but finally the horses were hitched up, the three travelers were settled into the buggy again, and they started off.

"I was hoping we'd get to Connorsville with a little time to spare for a few hours sleep," Mr. Court said. "But I doubt if that'll be possible, now."

Sheriff Bennett grunted. "This wild ride was your idea, Court," he reminded the newspaperman. "I was willing to telegraph to Granger to delay cutting for a day."

Mr. Court shook his head. "From what I know of Granger, a little thing like a telegram won't stop him. He can always claim they didn't send it out to the logging camp in time." He clucked to the horses, but when they broke into a trot he slowed them again. "Let's not take any chances," he said. "Better late than never."

It was true, thought Francie as she wrapped the carriage blanket around her against the chill of the night air. But late would be just the same as never for Carrie's tree. If they didn't make it to the logging camp before the cutting started everything would be for nothing. Carrie's beautiful tree, the oldest thing on earth, would be gone.

· Chapter Twenty ·

D awn was breaking as they trotted the tired horses through Connorsville. The loggers would be leaving camp by now, on their way to begin cutting Carrie's tree. "If I had not telegraphed to your parents," Court said to Francie, "I couldn't pass through town without notifying them. I told them we'd stop before we went up to the logging show, but there's not time, now." He looked back at Francie. "Sure you don't want us to let you off? You could just give us directions to the tree."

Francie was leaning forward in her seat, her hands pressed together in her lap. She kept her teeth clenched together to stop herself from shouting for Mr. Court to hurry. There wasn't a moment to spare. "Please," she said, swallowing her impatience. "I really want to be there."

Mr. Court nodded. "I guess you've got the right, since you found the will. However, I want you to stay in the buggy."

Francie caught her breath. In the buggy? "But I don't see how the buggy will be able to make it to Carrie's tree," she said. "The road's nothing but a slippery mountain track."

Sheriff Bennett held up his hand. "I say she can come with us, Court. I might need her as a witness." He turned to Francie. "But if you don't stay where I put you—then I *will* arrest you!" He drew his brows together in an awful frown.

"I promise," Francie answered, wondering if he was serious or not. She scooted a few inches away from him on the buggy seat. What a strange man.

Mr. Court drove the buggy up the road and through Connor's Basin. "You'll have to point out the way from here," he told Francie.

"It's not too far." Francie leaned out of the buggy window, watching for the beginning of the track leading up to Connor's Pass. "There." She pointed, and Mr. Court pulled the horses to a stop.

He got out and walked a few paces up the track. Then he came hurrying back. "You're right," he said to Francie. "The buggy would never make it." He tied the team to a nearby tree while Francie and Sheriff Bennett climbed out of the buggy.

"This way," Francie said, heading up the path. Her skirts kept wrapping around her legs, slowing her down. She kicked them out of her way and walked faster.

"Slow down, Miss Francie," Sheriff Bennett called to her. "It's not a race."

But it was a race, Francie wanted to argue. It was a race for the life of Carrie's tree. "It's still quite a way," she said instead, looking back at the men over her shoulder. "They'll be starting to work any moment."

Sheriff Bennett grunted. "They can't cut down the tree all in one day," he said.

"But they could make a big enough notch to kill it," Mr. Court pointed out. "Then they could argue they might as well cut it down." He had been charging up the hill only slightly behind Francie.

"Well," Sheriff Bennett drawled, "I hate to admit this," he said, "but this old man can't keep up with your pace. And since I'm the law around here, you might as well wait for me."

Francie ground her teeth together, but she stopped and waited for him to catch up. She patted the front of the borrowed shirtwaist, and then remembered that Mr. Court had taken the will for safekeeping. *Please let it be safe,* she prayed.

They passed the dogwood that marked Old Robert's cabin, and shortly afterward they heard the donkey engine's chugging. "They've started," Francie whispered. "They've already started!" She looked back to see Sheriff Bennett stop and lean against a tree to catch his breath. She felt like screaming.

When they reached the pass, Mr. Court and Francie were walking side by side, and as soon as they were on level ground, they both broke into a run. At the lip of the basin on the other side, Mr. Court stopped. Francie took a few steps down the path, but Mr. Court grabbed her arm and held her firmly. "Wait," he commanded. "Wait for Bennett."

The loggers had built a scaffolding around Carrie's tree about twenty feet high. This lifted the axmen above the enormous buttresses at the bottom of the trunk so they could start the undercut where the tree wasn't quite as thick. Even so, they had what seemed like a small army of men up on the platform. Two axmen were working on the undercut they'd begun chopping into the tree. The others were holding their axes as if waiting their turn.

Mr. Granger was up on the scaffolding beside the men, watching the axmen with his thumbs hooked into his suspenders. Francie thought the look on his face was smug and self-satisfied, like some kind of king overseeing his servants. He leaned over and said something to one of the axmen, and everyone laughed. Francie wished she could hear him. She didn't recognize any of the other men. So Charlie hadn't been chosen, she thought, wondering if he was glad or sorry.

She looked back as Sheriff Bennett came up behind them. "Well," he panted, "let's see what these fellows have to say about who owns this land." He turned to Francie.

"You stay here, Miss Francie. I want you safely out of any trouble."

He settled his hat firmly on his head and strode down the path, with Mr. Court behind him. No one even noticed them—all the loggers were intent on the cutting of Carrie's tree.

Francie watched them for a few moments, clenching and unclenching her fists. "I've got to be where I can hear," she mumbled. Nobody was looking in her direction. Silently she started down the path after them.

"Granger!" Sheriff Bennett shouted. "Lewis Granger! Call off your men for a moment."

Lewis Granger's head snapped around, eyes searching for the speaker. When he saw Sheriff Bennett, his smile was replaced by an expression that reminded Francie of an old stray dog they'd once cornered in the garbage bin behind the hotel. He looked both fearful and dangerous. But that so quickly turned into an angry frown that she blinked, not sure of what she had seen. Was he afraid of the sheriff?

Francie looked up as she felt a hand on her arm.

"Where have you been?" Charlie stepped in front of her. "The whole town's been looking for you. They're saying you rode the flume!"

"I had to," Francie told him. "I had to get to St. Joseph with Old Robert's will. To find out if it's real."

"You found the will?" Charlie's eyes were wide. He glanced at Granger and then back to Francie. "Granger says you broke into his cabin at the logging camp and stole something from him. He won't say what. He's saying you're no better than a street urchin. Your father is furious!"

Francie had to laugh. "At Granger or me?" She pushed on his arm. "You're blocking my way, Charlie. I've got to get down there."

He stepped aside and walked beside her, stopping just outside the ring of loggers who had gathered around the tree.

The axmen had stopped when they heard the sheriff's voice. "Keep working," Granger was shouting at them. "Or I'll dock your pay." He turned to the sheriff. "I'm in charge of this operation. I'll say when the men stop." He motioned to two of the axmen, who began again with their rhythmic chopping. Francie winced at each blow, as if the axes were chopping at her instead of the tree.

Sheriff Bennett began to climb up the scaffolding. Mr. Court stood at the bottom, his hand on the ladder as if he were deciding whether to go up or not. Then he stepped back and folded his arms to wait.

"You're all trespassing here," Sheriff Bennett roared at the men over the noise of the chopping and the donkey engine. "Any more damage to this property here and you'll all land in jail."

That stopped them. The axmen stepped back and looked at Granger.

"He's bluffing!" Granger shouted. "The Sierra Lumber Company owns this land, and everyone knows it."

"Turn that thing off!" Bennett motioned to the donkey engine, still chugging away, and a logger ran over to cut the motor. In the sudden silence, birds could be heard calling to one another.

Sheriff Bennett reached into his shirt pocket and brought out a paper, which he handed to Granger. "This is a copy of the deed to the 160 acres we are presently standing on. It runs from the other side of Connor's Pass to this side, and it includes this little valley and the trees you're in the process of cutting down. The owner is Robert Granger."

"Robert Granger's dead," Lewis Granger snorted. "I'm his brother. And as his only living relative, I'm his heir. So the land's mine."

"You'll agree, then, that Robert Granger owns this land?"

"He owned it. But on his death it reverted to me." He pulled himself up and stuck his thumbs into his suspender straps. "I sold it to the lumber company."

"How do you know he's dead?" Sheriff Bennett asked him. "He was a hermit and a roamer. The way I've heard it, he sometimes disappeared for months at a time. How do you know he hasn't shown up in St. Joseph this very day?"

Granger laughed. "He's dead. Take it from me."

Sheriff Bennett took a step closer to Granger. Francie held her breath—the platform wasn't very big. With one shove Granger could knock the sheriff off the edge—and it was a twenty-foot drop. She saw Mr. Court put his hand on the ladder and begin to climb up.

"Have you seen the body, Granger?" Sheriff Bennett kept his voice low, but everyone could hear him clearly.

Francie saw Granger's eyes flicker away from the sheriff. He licked his lips as if they were parched and dry. He has seen it! Francie's thoughts were spinning. He knows his brother is dead because he's seen the body. An image of the charred cabin timbers flashed into her mind. How could he know his brother was dead—how could he have seen the body, unless he'd been up there when the cabin burned? And why wouldn't he have said anything—brought his brother's body back for burial?

"What are you trying to say, Bennett?" Granger growled, but there was hesitation there, and fear. He looked like he was going to slug the sheriff. More than ever now he reminded Francie of that cornered dog.

"I'm just trying to get the facts straight," Sheriff Bennett said. Mr. Court had reached the top of the platform. Sheriff Bennett held out his hand and Mr. Court slapped a paper into it—it was the will.

But instead of opening it to show Lewis Granger, Sheriff Bennett reached into his other shirt pocket and pulled out a thin creamy piece of paper. "Before I left St.

Joseph," he said, unfolding it, "I telegraphed to Thomas Connor, asking him about this parcel of land. He confirms your statement. He even saw Robert Granger's will, dated September 16, 1885, leaving his land to you. He says you sold the land to Connor for five hundred dollars."

Granger's hands slipped back into the thumbs of his suspenders. He smiled. "So," he sneered, "how come you're here? Seems like everything's all correct and legal-like to me."

Now Sheriff Bennett unfolded the will. "I have here a will dated July 5, 1887—a later will than the one you showed Connor—leaving the land to a young lady, Mary Carolyn Cavanaugh."

Granger's face turned brick red. "Give me that," he croaked, grabbing the paper out of Bennett's hands. "You got this from the Cavanaugh brat. It's a forgery." He held it up and ripped it in two in front of the sheriff. "What do you think of your will now?" He opened his hands and let the two pieces of paper flutter to the platform.

Francie cried out, and then slapped her hands over her mouth. She saw Mr. Court turn around, and when he caught sight of her so close to the loggers, he raised his eyebrows. But nobody else even stirred. She felt Charlie's hand rest on her shoulder. "He tore it up!" she whispered.

"It must be on record," he whispered back. "Don't worry."

"It's not a forgery," Sheriff Bennett said, bending down

to pick up the torn will. "Mr. Court checked with the law firm you see listed here." He gestured to the paper. "By the way, no one seems to have heard of the law firm listed on the will you showed Connor. But for now I'll accept that it's a real will. And I'll accept, for the moment, that for some innocent reason known only to yourself, you know that your brother is dead and that you did nothing to hurry that death along." He tipped his hat back on his head. "But you're still trespassing. This land belongs to Mary Carolyn Cavanaugh or, rather, to her father, since she passed away shortly after this will was made. By the authority of the United States government, I order you off this land."

"We won't leave!" Lewis Granger almost jumped up and down on the platform. "I'll get permission from Cavanaugh. He'll sell me the land. He won't stand in my way. Send for Cavanaugh. Get him out here right now!"

Sheriff Bennett nodded to Mr. Court, who climbed down off the scaffolding and pushed his way through the crowd.

"I think he's already coming, boss," one of the loggers on the ground shouted. "Somebody went to get him when his daughter showed up here." The man nodded in Francie's direction and suddenly all eyes were turned on her.

"Hey, Francie," someone in the crowd called. "Did you really ride the flume to St. Joseph?" The question was greeted with cheers and whistles.

Francie's face burned. She wanted to turn and run, but Charlie's hand was tight on her shoulder. She stared straight ahead, trying not to look at anyone.

"They don't mean anything by it," Charlie whispered. "A lot of them bet on you to make it."

Francie closed her eyes. That made it even worse. Men betting on her! She would never live down the shame of it. Her parents would never forgive her. And it was all for nothing. Her father would sell the land to the lumber company. Carrie's tree was as good as down right now.

· Chapter Twenty-One ·

Francie perched on the edge of an old wagon bed. The oxen were hitched to the wagon, waiting patiently for their next instruction. She watched their tails twitching away flies.

Her eyes strayed to the pass—any moment her father would appear at the top of the path. He would stop, looking for her. And when he saw her sitting here with Charlie . . . her mind couldn't even imagine what he would do. Would he tell her she was no longer his daughter? That she had disappointed him too often? Would he say out loud what she knew he must wish in his heart, that she had been the one to die six years ago and that Carrie had lived instead? Carrie, who with all her wild ways, had never done anything like this. Carrie was trustworthy. Carrie . . . she slammed the heel of her boot on the side of the wagon. Carrie would have figured out a way to save the tree.

The wagon where they were sitting had been drawn halfway up the path to the pass. From here Francie could see the giant sequoia from top to bottom without even craning her neck. Without all the other trees around it, it seemed even bigger than it had on Sunday. The scaffolding around the bottom looked like something from a doll's house—so tiny was it in comparison with the tree's great size. The undercut the axmen had made was only a small notch, but it exposed the dark red heartwood of the tree and she could imagine the sap seeping into the wound, bleeding around the edges of the cut. Carrie was dead, and soon her tree would be dead, too. There would be nothing left of either of them.

"I wish we'd found it earlier," she said, hardly able to push the words out around the painful lump in her throat. "I wish I'd gotten to see it hundreds of times, to really appreciate it before it's gone." And she knew her wish was for Carrie, too. The diary was all she had left of her sister. It wasn't nearly enough.

Charlie put his arm around her and squeezed her shoulder. But there was nothing he could say to take away the sadness, and he didn't even try. Francie closed her eyes and leaned against him.

After a while she felt him straighten up. "He's coming," he whispered. He patted her shoulder once more and let his arm drop.

Francie looked up. Her father stood at the place where the path began to descend into the valley. He looked behind him, then walked back a few paces. And then her mother came into view. Her father took her mother's arm. They waited a moment, as if Francie's mother were catching her breath.

"Aunt Mary came!" Charlie sounded surprised, but somehow Francie was not. She slid off the wagon bed and watched them follow Mr. Court slowly down the path. For the first time she saw the gray streaks in her father's hair, and his shoulders were stooped in a way she hadn't noticed before. Her mother moved carefully, watching her feet, as if she were in pain. Francie bit her lip, wondering if they were hiding some illness from her. Or had she done this to them herself?

They stopped in front of her. "Francie . . ." her mother's voice caught on a half sob and she put out her hand. "We thought you were dead," she whispered.

Francie clasped her mother's hand in her own. "I'm fine," she said. She wanted to wrap her arms around her mother's shoulders, but she didn't dare.

"Thank you for taking care of her," Francie's father said to Mr. Court as the newspaperman stepped up beside them. His voice trembled slightly and he cleared his throat. Francie wondered if he were so angry he couldn't speak.

Mr. Court shook his head. "She can take care of herself," he answered with a small smile. "I don't think you need worry about Francie."

Francie felt her mother's hand tighten in her own, but her father's eyes narrowed as they rested again on Francie. That wasn't what he wanted to hear, but it's true, Francie thought, surprised. She remembered, belatedly, that she'd pulled her hair back in the style Carrie had favored, but she stopped herself from reaching up and pulling out the pins. Let him see how much she looked like Carrie. She stood up a little straighter and stared back at him.

"I'm sorry I worried you," she said, glancing from her father to her mother. She had to press her lips together to keep herself from going on, from trying to explain why she had to do it.

Her father nodded and exchanged a glance with her mother. Francie knew that look—it meant that he had more to say on the issue. But he only touched her shoulder and motioned her to walk beside him. "Let me do what I have to do, daughter," he said. "We want to get you home." He took her mother's arm once more and they walked down the path to Carrie's tree.

Francie could see her mother's gaze go up and up, and she heard her breath catch as she looked at the tree. Once she glanced at Francie with wide, wondering eyes. But her father stared straight ahead as if the tree were invisible to him.

Sheriff Bennett had been sitting on the ground underneath the scaffolding talking with the loggers. When he saw Francie and her parents he stood up. "Ah," he said, dusting off his hands. "Cavanaugh." He touched the brim of his hat and bobbed his head at Francie's mother. "Ma'am." Then he took Francie's father's arm and led him slightly aside. "Cavanaugh, you have some business to settle here, I believe. Did you know that old Robert Granger had willed his land to your daughter, Mary Carolyn?"

Francie's father cleared his throat. "I do now," he said. "Frank Court gave me the details."

Lewis Granger stomped over to them. He glared at Francie and ignored her mother. "Cavanaugh," he said, "the company will pay you five hundred dollars for this section of land. I can have a check to you by Monday."

Francie's mother made a small sound and put her hand over her mouth. Francie knew she was thinking about what they could do with that money at the hotel.

Her father glanced over at them and then back to Granger. "Five hundred dollars? That's quite a bit of money, Granger. I believe the company bought the rest of the land for one hundred dollars a section."

Granger swallowed, and Francie remembered that five hundred dollars was what he had received for the land himself—four hundred more than anyone else had!

"It's worth it to us," Lewis Granger answered. He hooked his thumbs under his suspenders and smiled at Francie's father.

"Father, please." Francie's heart was pounding in her throat so she could hardly speak. "Please. Don't do it."

She saw a spasm of pain cross her father's face and he looked down at her with unseeing eyes.

Francie's mother gripped her arm, and Francie turned to see that her face was creased with worry. "Francie, please," she begged. But then her eyes went to the tree again, and she shook her head. "I just don't know what's right," she whispered.

"Cavanaugh," Lewis Granger continued. "You've been a firm supporter of the company from the beginning, and you haven't been the worse for it. You'd never have made that hotel a success without the company." He looked at the men gathered around them and nodded, as if he were making up his mind about something. "Now I'm going to let you in on a fact that's not generally known. This depression has hurt us badly, and we've been forced to spend more than we could afford to keep this operation going. If we can't log this section it might put us under."

He stepped back and hid a small smile behind his hand. Francie thought he looked like a gambler playing a winning card. "That's crazy," she burst out. "You've logged the whole basin. How could these few acres make that much difference?"

The look Lewis Granger gave her was icy. "You shut up and leave this to your betters," he growled at her. "You've caused me enough trouble already. I've half a mind to put the law onto you!"

Francie saw her mother's head jerk up. Her father stiffened, and Francie was surprised to hear the anger she'd expected to be directed at her lash out at Granger instead. "Don't speak to my daughter like that, Granger," he said, and the cold warning in his voice was clear.

Granger stepped back. "I beg your pardon," he said, and he even gave a slight bow. "I didn't mean to give you any offense. But this is a decision for the adults to make, don't you agree, Cavanaugh?"

"I do," Francie's father answered. He put his hands in his pockets and stared down at his feet.

Francie held her breath, but when her father didn't look at her, she felt as if a lump the size of a boulder had settled into her stomach. Her mother was staring out at the devastation the loggers had made around Carrie's tree.

"I just don't see how I can be the one to put the company in the red," Francie's father said finally.

Francie couldn't let him finish. She grabbed his hands and spun around to face him. "Papa, I know I've disappointed you. I know you'd rather have Carrie here than me, but please, please, listen to me just this once." She looked up into his face, which was suddenly twisted into an expression of such pain and sadness it made her catch her breath. But she couldn't stop. "If you let them cut down this tree, it will be like Carrie dying all over again. Please, Papa, we can't have her back, but don't take this last part of her away from me." She held onto him as if she was drowning and he was the only lifeline.

Her father's face went white, as if she'd slapped him, and she realized that the crowd of loggers around them had become utterly silent. She turned to find that her mother had covered her face with her hands—her shoulders were shaking.

Francie felt as if someone had dumped a bucket of cold water over her. She closed her eyes. Once again, she'd crossed the line; she'd embarrassed them in front of everyone. Her father lifted his eyes to the men around them and then looked back at her. She saw his Adam's apple bob up and down as he swallowed.

"Francie," he whispered, using her nickname for the first time since Carrie died. "With all my heart I wish I had both you and Carrie here. I could never choose one over the other." He lifted a shaking hand and touched her hair. "You look so much like her . . ." he swallowed again, and she saw that his eyes were red with unshed tears. "When we couldn't find you yesterday . . . before we got Court's telegram, and I thought I'd lost you, too . . ." He took a breath that sounded like a sob. "I couldn't have borne it." He closed his eyes and pressed his lips together. He was gripping her hand as hard as she had been gripping his, and she felt, suddenly, that she was his lifeline, too.

"But I can't be the one to put the lumber company under," he continued. He let go of her hands. "It's not the money. It's not just my hotel. It's the jobs of all these men, too." He looked out at the loggers, and Francie heard shuffling as some of them shifted on their feet. "What else can I do?"

He was right. Francie knew it as soon as the words were spoken. If the company went broke, all those men would be out of work.

"Besides," Granger said, "this section is already cut. It's too late to save these trees—why not save jobs instead?" He patted the pocket of his shirt as if he were looking for his pen to write out the check then and there.

Granger had won and he knew it. Francie could hardly stand seeing that smug look on his face. She gritted her teeth and looked around the valley—once thick with growing pines. Now it looked like a desert—Carrie's tree was the only one left.

Her mother sighed, and her cheeks were wet with tears. "If there were only some way to turn back the clock—but the damage has already been done. We can't put the trees back."

Francie stared at her, and an idea suddenly blossomed in her mind. But would her father accept it? "Mama is right," she said slowly, turning to her father. "We can't put the other trees back. So why don't we sell them the wood they've cut already? We could even let them log the rest of the section as well—everything but Carrie's tree."

"That's preposterous!" Granger's face turned dark red. "The company has already paid for this lumber once. Paying again would put us even farther on the road to ruin!"

"And who did they pay it to last time?" Francie dug her fingernails into her palms to stop herself from shouting. "I think it was you!"

Francie's father put his hand on her shoulder. "Calm down, daughter," he said. "Let me handle this." He turned to Granger. "A moment ago you were offering me five hundred dollars for the lumber in this section." He folded his arms. "I believe I'm missing the point here."

"The point is," Granger spluttered, "that tree's half the wood in this section. Without it, the deal's no good to us. We'll go under and it'll be your fault. We've got to bring down that tree!"

Francie watched her father. His eyes narrowed, but his glance strayed to the loggers, standing grim and silent, and she knew he couldn't do it, couldn't take the money away from the company.

"Papa!" She grabbed his hand again to get his attention. "What if we give them the rest of the wood in the section. For free. Then it won't cost the company anything more than it did before. All they'd lose would be Carrie's tree."

Francie's father blinked and his eyebrows rose. "Give them the lumber? Is that good business sense?"

Francie wanted to scream, but she tried to keep her voice calm. "This isn't business! This is saving Carrie's tree without taking the loggers' jobs."

Francie's father stroked his mustache with his finger. Then he glanced at Granger.

"That tree's half the wood in this section," Granger said again. His jaw was set and his hands were balled into fists.

"If one tree's gonna make the difference between life and death for the company," one logger called out, "then I might as well quit right now!" Murmurs of agreement rippled through the crowd of men surrounding them.

"It seems like a fair deal to me," Mr. Court said, grinning. "And you'd save the company that five hundred dollars, too."

Francie's father gave Francie a long look. Then he looked at Francie's mother, and there was a light in his eyes Francie had not seen there in a long time. Francie's mother gave a slight nod. Then her father turned to Granger. "That's our offer, then. You can have the wood you've already cut and the rest of the lumber in this section free and clear, but you don't cut that tree. And we keep ownership of the land."

Granger's face was so red Francie thought he might burst. "I'll have to discuss it with Mr. Connor," he growled. He shoved the men nearest him aside and stomped off up the hill toward the pass.

"They'll take it," Sheriff Bennett said, watching Granger's back. "Granger can't afford to take a stand on this. I doubt if we could prove foul play in the death of his brother, but there's something very fishy about the whole thing. How does he know the man's dead? And why was he paid five times as much as anyone else for his section? He knows I'll be looking into it."

"Do you think he killed his own brother, then?" Mr. Court asked.

Sheriff Bennett stroked his chin with his fingers. "He's a mean one, but murder? I don't think he'd go that far."

Mr. Court shoved his hand in his pockets. "But the lumber company wanted this land. What if Old Robert refused to sell? Maybe there was a fight. Robert fell or hit his head—some kind of accidental death. Suddenly what Granger wanted to happen did happen—his brother is dead. Set the cabin on fire . . . a four-hundred-dollar bonus for his trouble . . ."

"Hold on, Court." Sheriff Bennett held up his hand. "Sounds like you're writing one of those dime novels to me. It makes me nervous when a newspaperman begins to speculate in advance of the evidence."

Mr. Court grinned. "Sorry," he said. "But if Connor accepts the Cavanaughs' offer it might be an indication of possible wrongdoing."

"Why wouldn't he accept it?" Sheriff Bennett asked. "Connor can't afford to turn down free lumber even without the wood in the big sequoia."

"We weren't sure we could bring that giant down in one piece, anyway," one of the loggers put in. He glanced at the tree, and his look was wistful. "Sure would've been fun to try, though."

"Looks like we get the rest of the day off, boys," Charlie said, slapping his hat on his thigh. "I think I'll go ride the flume into St. Joseph." He looked sideways at Francie as everyone laughed, and the crowd began to break up.

Francie flushed. "I'll never hear the end of that," she said under her breath.

"Not for a while," her mother answered. "I just hope those men don't break their necks trying to best you, Francie." She coughed and put her hand over her mouth, and Francie thought she might be concealing a smile.

"And there's also the matter of your punishment." Her father gave her a stern look. "Your mother and I can't condone that wild ride into St. Joseph, no matter how glad we are that you made it there safely."

Francie squared her shoulders, resolved not to argue no matter what the punishment was. But when she met his eyes, she saw that he was smiling. He smoothed her hair again with a hand that was still not quite steady. "Though I have no doubt that your sister would have been proud of you." He took her arm and they all walked together up toward the pass.

At the crest of the hill, Francie turned to look back at Carrie's tree. The loggers were dismantling the scaffolding. "The oldest tree on earth," she whispered, thinking about how many thousands of years it had stood surrounded by the quiet forest. Now it was alone. The trees in the valley were gone. Most of the other sequoias in the whole of Connor's Basin were gone. It had been the first tree, and now it was the last.

"I'm glad you saved it," her father said, touching her shoulder.

"You are?" She glanced up to see that he was still smiling. "Even with all the worry I caused you?"

"Even then." He reached down and, as if she were still only nine years old, he took her hand. She held her breath, realizing that he had not done that since Carrie died. Her hand felt small in his, warm and protected. "But I want you to promise," he added, "that you'll try to cause a little less trouble in the future."

Francie looked up at him, and turned to include her mother in her gaze, as well. She knew what she needed—what they all needed. "I will," she said, finally, "if you'll both promise to come here with me sometimes. I want to sit here and read to you from Carrie's diary."

She saw the shadow pass over her father's face, and her mother bit her lip. She put her hand to her collar, and Francie knew she wanted to say no, to hide from the pain it would cause. But at last they both nodded. Her father cleared his throat. "We'll all come together. I promise."

"Good." She knew, then, that it would happen.

· Author's Note ·

Before 1890 the area west of Kings Canyon National Park known as the Converse Basin was home to the finest stand of Sierra redwood trees (also known as sequoias) in the United States—some say it was the finest stand on earth. Between 1890 and 1903, the entire basin was logged. You can drive through Converse Basin. You can still see the stumps of these huge trees, and the ones that shattered when they hit the ground.

At the far north end of Converse Basin stands the Boole Tree. It was discovered when logging in the area was drawing to a close, and it was believed to be the largest and possibly also the oldest tree on earth. (More recent measurements have shown it to be third largest in bulk, though it has the largest circumference—112 feet with a base diameter of 35 feet.) Though preparations were made to log the tree, it was never cut. Some say it was simply too big—it couldn't be brought down and moved without shattering the brittle wood. Others say that conservationists engineered a trade—the saving of the Boole Tree in exchange for easier to log timber on nearby land. The true answer will probably never be known.

At the time of its discovery, all the trees around the Boole Tree were cut. Old photos show the lone giant standing amid the rubble of downed trees. But today, one hundred years later, the Boole Tree is no longer alone. If you take the mile hike, as I have, up over a steep hill and down the other side, you will find it surrounded by new generations of pine and firs, and even a number of thin and willowy sequoias, still in their infancy, but healthy and strong.

I've been fascinated with sequoias for many years, since I read *The Biggest Living Thing* by my friend and fellow children's writer, Carolyn Arnold. From that book and from my later research I learned that the first white man to see a sequoia was a hunter named A. T. Dowd. He found the tree in what is now the Calaveras Big Trees State Park in about 1852. Only a year later, in 1853, it was cut down because people wanted to find out its age. It was, they learned, more than two thousand years old. When I learned this I was outraged at the arrogance of humankind, of people who thought it was proper to kill something that had been in the world for two thousand years simply to find out how old it was.

It was with that sense of outrage that I began the research that led, more than ten years later, to *Riding the Flume*. I learned much about logging and loggers, and now I find my outrage tempered with a kind of awe and even grudging respect for the men who had the daring and confidence to pit their tiny selves and their even tinier axes against the giants. It is amazing to me that they would even imagine that they could cut down a sequoia—more than three hundred feet tall and sometimes much more than twenty feet in diameter—with an ax. But they did imagine it. They even attempted it. And they succeeded.

It is a fact worth pondering—humans are, without a doubt, the most powerful species in the world. We can destroy a species much bigger and stronger than we are. It is only our awareness of that power, and our resolve to use it responsibly, that will stop us from destroying the earth.

· Glossary ·

axmen: the men who began the process of cutting down a tree. With broad, swinging strokes of their double-bitted axes, they chopped a triangular-shaped notch on one side of the tree.

chute: a dry wooden track running along the ground on which logs were slid from the woods to a landing. The logs were chained together in long lines and dragged along the chute by oxen or by the cables attached to a donkey engine.

chute rider: The man who rode on top of the last log in the line as the logs were pulled down the chute. Sometimes logs would rear up in the track, fall off the track, or even catch on fire from friction. Then the chute rider would touch the telegraph wires near the chute with a metal-tipped pole to signal the man running the donkey engine about what was happening and whether to slow down or speed up the log train.

crosscut saw: a saw with a long thin blade with teeth on one side. The kind used in the California logging operations usually had a handle on each end. Two men were needed to draw the saw back and forth and cut into the tree trunk.

donkey steam engine: a portable steam engine with cables attached. It was used to pull logs through the woods to a central location where they were loaded onto railroad cars and taken to the mill. It replaced the teams of oxen used to perform the same task.

double-bitted ax: an ax with a sharpened edge on either side of the metal head.

fallers: the men who did the work of cutting down or "felling" the trees.

featherbed: also called a "felling bed"—a pile of small trees and branches arranged beside the tree to cushion it when it fell and hopefully keep it from shattering.

flume herders: the men who lived in small houses built at regular intervals along the flume route. They monitored the lumber floating down the flume, broke up log jams, and repaired leaks.

logging show: the logging operation in the woods . . . cutting the trees and transporting them to the mill.

lumber flume: a U-shaped or V-shaped trough built above the ground on a framework or scaffolding. The flume looked a bit like a roller coaster and the trough had several feet of water flowing through it. It was, in essence, a man-made stream or river built above the ground and used to move lumber from mills high in the mountains to other locations at lower elevations.

picaroon: (also spelled pickaroon) a long pole with a hook on one end. The flume herders used picaroons to help maneuver the lumber down the flume.

sawmill: where logs were sawed into boards by machinery.

sawyers: the men who wielded the crosscut saw. Standing one on either side of the tree, they drew the saw back and forth, making a cut that was parallel to the ground. They always began the cut on the side of the tree that was opposite to the undercut. The men who worked in the mill saw-ing the logs into boards and planks were also called sawyers.

skidroad: a path through the woods used for dragging logs. The skidroad was also that part of a lumber town where most of the saloons were built—loggers went there to drink during their free time. The expression "on Skid Row" which means "poor and out of work," later devel-oped from this logging term.

undercut: a triangular notch cut by the axmen in one side of the tree. The undercuts in sequoia trees were often big enough for a man on horseback to stand up inside the notch.

wedges: large pieces of triangular-shaped steel hammered into the slice cut by the crosscut saw. This kept the weight of the tree from resting on the saw and trapping it in the trunk.

· For Further Reading ·

Here are a few of the books I used in researching the discovery and logging of the redwood trees in California.

Andrews, Ralph. *Redwood Classic*. New York: Bonanza Books, 1958. This book talks about the early days of logging in California.

Dilsaver, Larry M., and William C. Tweed. *Challenge of the Big Trees: A Resource History of Sequoia and Kings Canyon National Parks*. Three Rivers, Calif.: Sequoia Natural History Association, Inc., 1990. This book focuses on the human story around the creation of these national parks.

Johnston, Hank. *They Felled the Redwoods: A Saga of Flumes and Rails in the High Sierra*. Fish Camp, Calif.: Stauffer Publishing, 1996. Go to this book for fabulous photos of the sequoias and learn how they were cut down.

Peattie, Donald Culross. *A Natural History of Western Trees*. Boston: Houghton Mifflin Co., 1953. Biological information on the trees. His description of sequoias captures their quiet majesty.

Sargent, Shirley. *Pioneers in Petticoats: Yosemite's Early Women 1856–1900*. Yosemite, Calif.: Flying Spur Press, 1966. This book will give you a good idea of the unconquerable spirit of the women who helped settle California.

Seagraves, Anne. *Women of the Sierra*. Hayden, Idaho: WESANNE Publications, 1990. Short biographies of the women who lived in the Sierra Nevada mountains between 1840 and 1890.

Zauner, Phyllis. *Those Spirited Women of the Early West: A Mini-History*. Sonoma, Calif.: Zanel Publications, 1994. More biographies of the strong women of California and the West.